Joseph, Rachel's son

Mark Morgan

Bible
Tales
www.BibleTales.online

Published in Australia, by Bible Tales Online.
www.BibleTales.online

Joseph, Rachel's son

ISBN (Paperback): 978-1-925587-30-2
ISBN (eBook): 978-1-925587-31-9

Cover picture: On the Banks of the Nile, Upper Egypt
by John Frederick Lewis (1876).

Free Download

Paul in Snippets

An 81-page PDF novelette by Mark Morgan.

The life of Paul painted from the Acts of the Apostles.

Get your free copy of *Paul in Snippets* when you sign up for the Bible Tales mailing list. As well as the eBook, you will receive a weekly email newsletter with micro tales, informative articles and special offers.

Visit **https://www.BibleTales.online/free-pins**

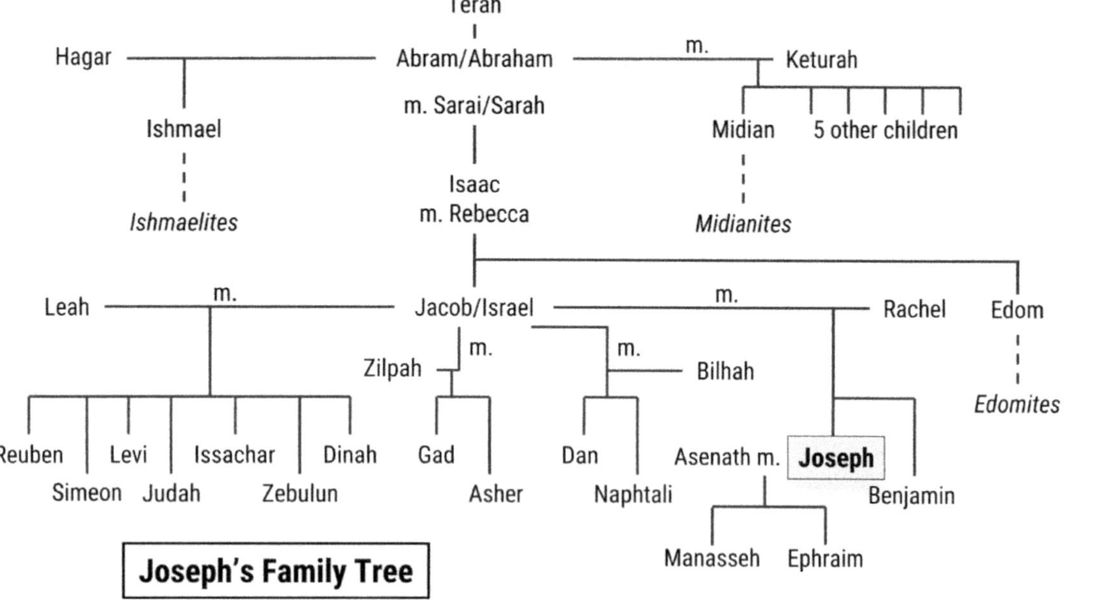

Joseph's Family Tree

To my ever-patient wife, Ruth.

Acknowledgements and thanks

In mid-2017, two of my children introduced me to NaNoWriMo[1], and I decided to write a story about one of my favourite Bible characters – Joseph.

Writing 50,000 words in 30 days was hard. At midnight on 30 November 2017, I was sitting in the tiny hamlet of Navarre (Victoria, Australia), still typing desperately – in the middle of a sentence. Word count: 50,004, with 22,000 words in the last four days. The story was still unfinished and demanded several months of extra work, but I doubt that I would have started yet without NaNoWriMo.

Chapter 8 "Dinah", first appeared as a micro-tale in the Bible Tales Online weekly newsletter. Minor changes were made to merge it into this story.

The map of Mesopotamia on page 4 was derived from a map by Yiyi[2] of the Middle East[3] with a CC BY 3.0[4] licence.

Particular thanks go to Ruth, my wife, who always helps me find time to write, and then patiently reads it all.

My oldest daughter, Cathy, has proofread the manuscript several times, making countless corrections and improvements. Thanks, Cathy.

A request

If you find any typos, spelling errors, poor grammar, unkempt use of vocabulary, or places where the story misrepresents the Bible, please let me know. I can't correct printed books, but electronic versions and new printed copies can be fixed.

---

[1] National Novel Writing Month (https://nanowrimo.org/)

[2] https://commons.wikimedia.org/wiki/User:Yiyi

[3] https://commons.wikimedia.org/wiki/File:Near_East
_topographic_map_with_toponyms_3000bc.svg

[4] https://creativecommons.org/licenses/by/3.0/deed.en

Contents

Figures

God was with him...

And the patriarchs,
jealous of Joseph,
sold him into Egypt;
but God was with him

Acts 7:9

And the LORde was with Ioseph
and he was a luckie felowe
and continued in the house
of his master the Egiptian.

Genesis 39:2 (Tyndale)

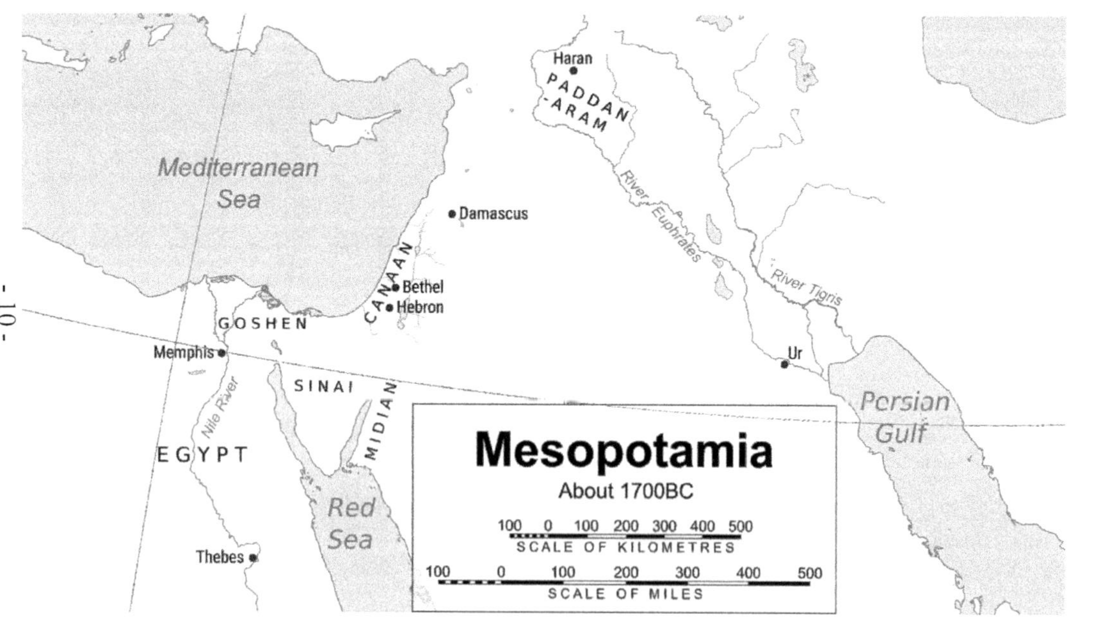

Mesopotamia
About 1700BC
100 0 100 200 300 400 500
SCALE OF KILOMETRES
100 0 100 200 300 400 500
SCALE OF MILES
Mediterranean Sea
Haran
PADDAN -ARAM
River Euphrates
River Tigris
Damascus
CANAAN
Bethel
Hebron
GOSHEN
Memphis
Nile River
SINAI
MIDIAN
EGYPT
Red Sea
Thebes
Ur
Persian Gulf

Chapter 1

Escape from Haran

For a six-year-old, it was an exciting time – the most exciting day of his life. But it was also confusing. Everybody except him seemed to understand what was going on, but all he knew was that they were leaving – leaving the only place he had ever known as home.

The children had all been woken in the early dawn so that the tents could be packed up. A dozen dazed and sleepy children wandering around asking questions was never going to be easy to handle, so Jacob's plan had been for Leah to take care of them all, sitting quietly near the heavily-laden camels, while everyone else packed and loaded the rest of the family's goods.

But it didn't work out quite like that. Leah did her best of course, but after a while there were children everywhere: running, walking, pushing, shouting – and getting under everybody's feet. After all, it was much too exciting a morning for anyone to sit still!

Laban was away – well, yes, of course he was; that's why Jacob's family was leaving at that time, and the chief reason for Jacob's urgency, too. Laban and his sons had gone to shear his sheep, and would not be back until all the sheep were shorn. Jacob guessed that he had two or three days, or maybe even four with the way that Laban's flocks had grown.

Jacob was desperate to leave. Already the time was running away. It was no longer early morning, yet still the servants were busy bundling up the tents and tying them on the camels' backs. Maidservants had packed the pots and pans, the cooking utensils and the hand mills for grinding, as well as the bedding, clothing, curtains, mats, and more things than Jacob could ever have imagined. Countless items, small and large, had accumulated over the twenty years he had spent in Haran. Every extra person added to the family had brought extra needs, likes and dislikes, and the family baggage had increased accordingly. Now it all had to be carried away. Or abandoned – left to enrich Laban a little more. And Jacob didn't want that. Over the last few months, Laban's selfish and greedy behaviour had preyed on his mind more and more – the deceit and trickery, the domination and manipulation. Whatever else happened, Jacob did not want to make him any richer. If God hadn't been looking after him, Jacob knew that Laban would never have let him leave at all, save as he had come – with nothing.

He thought back to his arrival: one man alone, walking into the lives of his relatives in search of a wife. Not that he had told them so. But Laban remembered the expedition sent by Abraham to find a wife for Isaac, Jacob's father, and Jacob was sure that Laban had begun to make plans the first time he laid eyes on him. Plans to use him, exploit him, cheat him and completely control him.

But now, Jacob was leaving. Taking his own and leaving Laban with all that was his. No more, no less. And they must hurry.

Menservants looked after the camels, donkeys, sheep and goats, as well as the heavy goats'-hair tents with all of their poles, ropes and pegs. Packing, tying, balancing, adjusting – and above all, hurrying. Well before everyone else was ready, the sheep and goats set out, led from in front and driven from behind by Jacob's experienced herdsmen. He worried about not being with them, but they would not be able to travel as quickly as everyone else.

Jacob had tried to make sure there were enough camels and donkeys, but too many would have raised Laban's suspicions, so there weren't as many as he would have liked. Still, they made an impressive array when they were all gathered together. The main thing was that everyone must have a mount, even if it meant they had to leave other things behind. Each day must take them as far away from Laban as possible.

Packing was almost complete and it was time to arrange the children and their mothers. Leah still had four of her sons with her, and Dinah was at her side as always. Where were the other two? Ah, there: Simeon and Levi, together as usual, and doing their best to help a servant with tying the last tent onto a camel who wasn't cooperating.

And Rachel, lovely Rachel, where was she? He still found it hard to keep his eyes off her, but this morning was a special case, and for the moment he didn't know where she was. Joseph, Rachel's son, was there, standing quietly, holding the halter of the camel on which he and his mother would ride. Even at six years old, Joseph could be relied on to be where you needed him, but Rachel was not there.

"Joseph," Jacob called urgently, "where is your mother?"

"She just went back to Grandpa's house. She said she would be back soon. In fact, here she comes now." He spoke in a high-pitched, boyish voice, but his speech was always quite grown-up.

Rachel, her long dark hair framing the beautiful face that had kept Jacob in Haran so many years, was hurrying towards them.

"Are we ready to leave, Jacob?" she asked, a little breathlessly. She was carrying some small bags that looked quite heavy, and quickly tucked them into pockets on the side of the camel's saddle.

"It looks like it," replied Jacob. "But I just need to check that everyone is ready." He moved away and checked on Leah's maid Zilpah and Rachel's maid Bilhah, each with her two sons. Although the boys were only a little older than Joseph, they would travel in pairs on camels of their own. Jacob hoped they would be alright that way. The camels he had chosen for them were calm, serene beasts of advanced age, but those lads were much too good at finding trouble, particularly Gad and Asher, Zilpah's sons.

His wives and children were all ready, but some of the servants were still running around, making sure that everything was properly packed.

All of the pack animals had been fed and the camels had been given as much water as they wanted. The herdsmen travelling with the sheep and goats had already left: they knew that this journey would not be a slow and easy expedition. Jacob had made it clear to everyone that not a moment was to be wasted. Any speed that the animals could endure, they must endure. His wives knew this too, although Jacob suspected they didn't yet understand quite how important it was, or realise how much speed he would demand of them.

They would find out soon enough.

Finally, everyone was ready and mounted on camels or donkeys. Joseph sat with his mother on their camel's back and watched as his father Jacob, long beard stirring a little in the breeze, prepared to lead off. A good lead camel makes it easier for other camels to follow, and the large bull camel that Jacob rode was a good leader. He had a regal bearing and firm opinions of what he wanted to do. At that moment, he did not want to leave. Possibly he sensed somehow that this departure would be a permanent separation, or maybe it was just the general excitement that had infected him. Whatever the reason, it took all of Jacob's considerable skill with camels to convince him to set out. Slowly, the rest of the camels and donkeys wended their way through the gate, following Jacob on his softly pacing beast. A group of menservants brought up the rear. As the last one passed through the gate, he halted his camel, climbed down and quietly closed the gate.

They were off. An impressively large group – but only one, Jacob, knew where they were going. Jacob was returning home.

Chapter 2

On the run

Joseph remembered that first night for the rest of his life. The excitement of their hurried flight from Haran while Grandpa was away shearing had caught his imagination, and his father's constant insistence that they must not delay added to the sense of mystery.

He couldn't understand why they had to hurry away, nor why they should leave without telling Grandpa.

Just a few of the tents were put up that night, so the sleeping arrangements were rather crowded. All eleven of the boys were in one small tent, and Joseph listened to the chatter and gossip of his half-brothers with some interest. Clearly, they'd heard much more about what was happening than his mother had told him.

"Grandpa says he is going to kill Daddy," said ten-year-old Simeon, breathlessly.

"Oh, don't be silly," responded twelve-year-old Reuben, loftily. "He wouldn't do that. We're just leaving because Daddy wants to see his parents."

"Well," put in ten-year-old Levi, "Adah told me that Grandpa and Daddy don't get on, and we're leaving so that there won't be any more arguments."

The discussion continued, with the suggested reasons for their departure ranging from homesickness to plans of religious massacres.

After a while, Joseph slipped out of the tent and sat outside, looking at the stars. There were so many to see, and they always reminded him of the promise his father had told him about. Abraham, Jacob's grandfather, had been given a promise that he would have as many descendants as the stars in the heavens! One night when Joseph had been only five, Jacob had sat with him in Haran looking up at the stars, and told him to try counting them. He had tried, but it was so hard to remember which ones you had already counted, and even with Jacob's help, he had only been able to get to twelve before he couldn't be sure any more whether or not he had already counted that next star.

Jacob had laughed at him, softly, then explained about God's promise and said that Abraham already had more than twelve descendants, but that there were a lot more stars than that. Jacob had told Joseph that he had tried counting the stars himself when he was about Joseph's age, while his grandfather Abraham was still alive, and how Abraham had told him so confidently that God's promise would come true.

Jacob had many stories to tell about Abraham and his friendship with El Shaddai, the God of the Hebrews, and Joseph wanted to hear them all. But tonight Jacob was at the campfire with his wives and Joseph was all alone in a camp full of people. He couldn't believe all that his brothers were saying about his grandfather, although he knew that some of the comments were true. He couldn't quite understand why, but it was clear that Grandpa and Daddy did not get on well, and he was fairly sure that none of his mothers liked Grandpa much either. Joseph himself, however, quite enjoyed the time he spent with the abrupt and often irritable old man.

Grandpa had lots of stories to tell too, and Joseph was not yet old enough to notice that most of them had a common thread of deception and intrigue. He was also unaware that Laban understood very well that Joseph was Jacob's favourite son and had found that he could often learn how Jacob was feeling and what his plans were by talking to Joseph. Laban's way of operating was always more successful if he knew what his victims were planning. Jacob knew Laban's methods and had warned his wives about the problem, forbidding them from discussing him with Laban. After that, Laban had tried the children and found that Joseph was the most useful one to pump for information. At the same time, he'd also found that he actually enjoyed the child's company and quite admired his ideas of right and wrong – not that he would ever have followed them himself!

Joseph leaned sleepily back against one of the tent poles and wondered whether he would ever see Grandpa again. He had asked his mother that question as they had travelled that day and she had said it was not likely: Grandpa was an old man, although he was still very fit. Even with the excitement of running away, it had been a long day's riding, and Joseph was tired as he looked up at the stars again and did his best to count them.

When Jacob did the rounds of the camp later that night, he found Joseph asleep, still leaning against the tent pole. Picking him up, he carried him into the tent and laid him on his mat, giving him a kiss on the cheek as he left. All of the other boys were asleep too, and Jacob went out to continue his inspection.

Finally back in his own tent, Jacob wondered uneasily whether they had travelled far enough that day. Would Laban chase them? Rachel and Leah didn't believe that he would, but Jacob wasn't so sure. He knelt down and prayed to the God who had told him to return to Canaan.

Chapter 3

Pursuit

Jacob was relentless. Every day, the flocks and herds left the camp at dawn, well before the tents were packed up. At some time during the day, the quicker-moving main party would catch up with the animals and then leave them behind. Every evening, the flocks and herds caught up with the rest at about sunset, arriving just in time for them to be cared for before the darkness was complete. The servants were told they must not over-drive the animals, but neither could they let them waste any time.

Nobody else had any time for rest either. Camels can keep up a swift pace for hours on end, and that was what Jacob expected of them. The donkeys found the going much harder, though, and their drivers were doing their best to slow down the march so that they weren't overtaxed.

Jacob had concluded that Laban would probably not find out until the third day that they had left Haran, and he was determined to put as great a distance between them as possible by then. He knew just how hard he could push the cattle, sheep and goats, and he meant to get every possible step out of them. If Laban was angry enough to follow on the first day, Jacob wanted him to find that the distance they had travelled was so great that he would give up. If the first day didn't achieve that, he hoped that the second and third would do so.

By the time they set up camp on the third day, he was quite pleased with the distance they had covered overall. But he knew that Laban would probably have arrived back in Haran and discovered their absence. What would he do?

Jacob calculated that if Laban got straight onto his camel and pursued them, driving the beast as hard as he could, he would catch up with them in about five to ten days. Jacob judged that the ninth, tenth and eleventh days of their journey would be the most risky, and made plans to ensure that a good guard was kept on those days – but without worrying his wives or children.

If Laban was angry and determined enough to continue the chase until he caught them, there was no way of telling what he might do, or try to do.

◌◌

The ninth day dawned clear and calm, and Jacob made sure there was a guard at the back. It seemed a little foolish, but he made sure that the guards were armed. Throughout the day, he kept scanning the horizon behind for telltale signs of pursuit.

But there was nothing, and when the camp was set up for the night, Rachel told him quietly that she was confident her father would not come. Leah talked to him during the evening meal too, and observed that there were no signs of pursuit. She too was confident that they had escaped her father's web of intrigue and hinted that they would enjoy a more sedate journey from then on.

"No, Leah," Jacob replied. "We can't take it easy yet. If we still haven't seen your father in two days' time, then I will feel easier, but not until then."

It was late on the tenth day when Jacob saw the tiny cloud of dust far behind them as they climbed a small hill. Never mind, he thought, it must be travellers. Other travellers. Not Laban.

All the same, he urged everyone to hurry up.

"We've been making good time," he said to his chief servant, "but it would be good if we could get just a little bit further before we stop for the night."

They hurried on, and the cloud of dust was still a long way off when they had to make camp for the night.

The animals were still some distance behind them, and whoever was making that cloud of dust would soon catch up with them. If it was Laban, he would recognise the servants and possibly even the animals, all mottled and spotted as they were.

Never mind, Jacob thought to himself, it's probably not Laban anyway.

Chapter 4

Confrontation

It was Laban, and he was fuming as he rode into the camp on his strong, swift camel with his sons and his kinsmen at his side. His hair was dusty and windswept, but the wind of his whirlwind journey had clearly not cooled his temper. He was furious and he didn't care who knew it.

"What do you mean by it, Jacob?" he barked. "All this sneaking and running away?"

It was a hard question to answer without upsetting him even more, and Jacob was loth to do that.

"Can we talk about it tomorrow?" Jacob suggested.

"Why should we wait?" snorted Laban. "Let's have it out now! What have you done, that you have tricked me and driven away my daughters like captives of the sword?"

"Hardly that," protested Jacob. "You can see that they are all here, free to go where they will."

"Why did you flee secretly and trick me? You waited until I was away shearing, and did not tell me. I could have sent you away with laughter and songs, with tambourine and lyre."

"We wanted to leave quietly and peacefully," Jacob replied in a soothing voice, but Laban was in no mood to be soothed.

"And why did you not permit me to kiss my sons and my daughters farewell?" complained Laban, gesturing towards the women and children who were all standing around listening to this diatribe.

"I would have done so if…" began Jacob.

"You have done foolishly," interrupted Laban, moving his magnificent camel close to where Jacob stood and looking down on him angrily.

"It is in my power to do you harm," he said threateningly, and the boys looked at each other. Maybe the worst of the suggestions they had heard were about to come true. Then Laban leaned forward and shook his head in disgust: "But the God of your father spoke to me last night, saying, 'Be careful not to say anything to Jacob, either good or bad.' "

Jacob was relieved to hear it, but he couldn't help wondering what Laban's words so far had been if they weren't "either good or bad".

Laban stopped for a minute, took a deep breath, and seemed to grow a little less agitated. "And now you have gone away because you longed greatly for your father's house," he continued more calmly; but then the anger burst out again: "but why did you steal my gods?"

This was a completely unexpected accusation, and, Jacob felt, utterly unjust. He was not interested in Laban's gods, and would never have accepted them even if Laban had given them to him!

"What do you mean?" Jacob asked, stalling for time.

"My gods," Laban repeated, "the ones from the house. When we returned home, they were gone. The servants said they had not been seen since you left."

Jacob looked around at his family and then at Laban's formidable sons and relatives, and said to Laban, "I left as we did because I was afraid, for I thought that you would take your daughters from me by force. But I did not take your gods."

"Then maybe someone else stole them," suggested Laban. "They were certainly gone once your family had left."

"Anyone with whom you find your gods shall not live," said Jacob boldly, confident that there was nothing to be found. "In the presence of our kinsmen, point out what I have that is yours, and take it."

Jacob did not notice Rachel's sudden start when he condemned the thief to death, but Joseph, standing quietly beside his mother, did. Looking up at her, he saw fear in her eyes, though he was not old enough to guess the reason immediately.

Laban inclined his head in agreement, made his camel kneel and climbed down, ready to search Jacob's goods.

As soon as Laban entered Jacob's tent, Rachel sidled over to her tent, taking Joseph with her. She entered the tent and walked over to the saddle that sat on the floor near the back of the tent. Quickly she reached into one of the small pockets on the side and felt around urgently, then looked relieved as her hand evidently found what it sought. Swiftly, she arranged herself on the saddle so that it looked as if she had chosen it as a comfortable place for an exhausted woman to sit, adjusting her skirts carefully so that they covered the side of the saddle and hid the pockets.

"Joseph, my son," she said quite calmly, although her eyes still betrayed her concern, "come and sit beside me, down there on the floor."

"Why, Mother?"

"Because I want to tell you a story while we are waiting, Joseph. How about a… a story of the time when I met your father? Would you like that?"

"Oh, yes please!" said the boy, sitting down quickly. "I always like to hear that one."

"One day, I was out in the fields looking after Grandpa's flocks – since I was a shepherdess, as you know," began Rachel. Joseph had heard the story many times, but he was always ready to hear it again: how his mother had been the first to meet his father when he had arrived in Haran, twenty years before. How Jacob had immediately kissed her and then stayed and worked for Laban for seven long years so that he could marry her.

As always, Rachel told the story carefully, highlighting certain parts and glossing over the parts that were better left out. Perhaps when Joseph was grown up she could tell him more, but maybe some history was best left in the past. There was no need to mention her utter devastation that day – the day that should have been her wedding day – when Laban had told her that Jacob would be marrying her older sister Leah instead of her. Laban had arranged to have her taken away to visit a distant relative for the day so that she was far away when Jacob was tricked into marrying Leah. Leah and Rachel were very similar in height and figure, and a carefully arranged veil had hidden Leah's face from a deluded Jacob.

Skipping over all those details, both the ones that hurt so much to tell and those that would hurt her sister Leah at least as much, she skipped to the game that they often played in this story, the game of guessing the order of his brothers' births.

Who was the oldest? Well, that was easy: Reuben. And who was Leah's youngest? Oh, much harder. Joseph's eyes screwed up in concentration and he was still thinking hard when Jacob and Laban walked into the tent.

Laban had searched through everything in Jacob's tent, but had not found his gods. He had then searched Leah's tent, the tent that Bilhah and Zilpah shared, the tent of the boys' and those of the servants with an equal lack of success. By the time he followed Jacob into Rachel's tent, he was looking less confident, while Jacob was looking more and more furious.

"The last one," said Jacob, speaking to Laban more sharply than Rachel had ever heard him do before.

"I'm sorry, father," said Rachel, as Laban walked into the tent. "I can't get up at the moment – ah, I'm a woman, you know."

"That's alright," answered Laban, awkwardly.

Jacob waved his arm abruptly at the goods in the tent – almost all parcelled up. They were travelling, and everything would need to be ready for travel again the next morning. Laban knew what he was looking for – precious, solid and heavy metal idols. The good luck charms of his house. These were the gods in which he trusted to keep his home and family safe, and Jacob secretly felt that it was really only these that had brought Laban so far on such an arduous trek.

Laban felt over each parcel and package, checking the weight and pressing to see if the feel of cold hard metal would reward his searching fingers. At times, a solid item met his touch through the cloth, and once his heart leapt as he felt a heavy, rounded object, but it took little detailed examination to scuttle his hopes again as he recognised a small hand mill for grinding grain.

Slowly, he worked his way around the outside of the tent and came up empty-handed. Nothing at all to show for seven exhausting days of hard riding – he began to feel his age. Was there anywhere else he could look? He slowly straightened and turned towards Rachel.

He knew his daughters, and as he met Rachel's eyes, he thought he saw, ever so briefly, a fleeting look of triumph, although it disappeared as quickly as it had come.

His suspicions were roused at once and he took a hasty step towards her, about to ask what she was hiding. But she was no longer the pretty younger daughter from whom he could demand cooperation. She was a married woman, a mother, and maybe an expectant mother – if that was what her veiled comment had meant. He noticed for the first time that she was sitting on a camel's saddle. Joseph, his favourite grandson, was sitting quietly by her and looking up at him with large, dark, frightened eyes. Laban felt some sympathy for the child – he must have frightened him with his anger and talk of stealing.

Laban looked again at Rachel, who looked back at him boldly enough, but with a little discomfort in her eyes. Maybe he had imagined that fleeting look. But he still wanted to search that saddle. His gods had not been anywhere else, and that saddle was the last place he could look.

"Mother," asked Joseph, "can I answer now? I've worked it out."

"Yes, my dear," said Rachel, looking at him with love, and maybe also with thankfulness for the distraction.

"Zebulun," he answered confidently.

"You're right, of course," replied Rachel with a smile. "Do you think Grandpa could answer the question?" She looked up at Laban with that entrancing smile in her eyes that had always made her so attractive.

"What question?" Laban asked, a little irritably, but unable to resist those eyes.

"Why, who was Leah's youngest son?" Rachel's tone was one of innocent enquiry.

"Well, Joseph has already given the answer, but I would have known it anyway."

"Would you?" her eyes teased him. "Then who is Leah's fifth son, father?"

"Oh, you and your questions," he replied gruffly, then turned and walked out of the tent.

Jacob followed him, and Rachel and Joseph were left alone in the quiet tent. Rachel closed her eyes, leaned forward and put her face in her hands, looking exhausted. Joseph was still looking up at her and asked in concern, "What's wrong, Mother?"

"Nothing, nothing," she replied wearily, pushing back the long hair that had fallen across her face. "I'm just tired."

"Will Grandpa get his lucky idols back, Mother? Could we help him find them?"

"If Grandpa can't find them himself, how could we help him?" she answered carefully. Joseph often surprised her with what he understood, but surely this would be beyond even him, wouldn't it? He was only a little boy.

"I just wondered, Mother. Grandpa seems so upset to have lost them."

She looked at him thoughtfully, trying to come up with a way to find out what he knew without giving things away if he didn't know anything.

Suddenly, there came the sound of raised voices outside. Jacob was obviously taking Laban to task. So much anger had accumulated over twenty years of mistrust and deception – Laban was dumbfounded. He had never heard Jacob so angry and outspoken before. The words tumbled out and Laban was forced, for once, to listen to a most unflattering assessment of his actions and motives. Jacob listed his grievances: the ten changes of wages, the harsh work conditions, the demanding of payment for any injured or lost livestock, the insult of chasing them from Haran to the hills of Gilead like runaway slaves, and finally the wrongful accusation of stealing. Jacob's speech left Laban almost at a loss for words, but his arrogance and robust self-confidence stopped him from being overwhelmed – and probably from learning a lesson that would have done him good!

In the tent, Joseph still watched Rachel with wide eyes as Jacob and Laban angrily agreed to go each his own way. And he looked sad. This night too would live in his memory – a night of drama and fear, of shouting and anger, of deception and uncertainty.

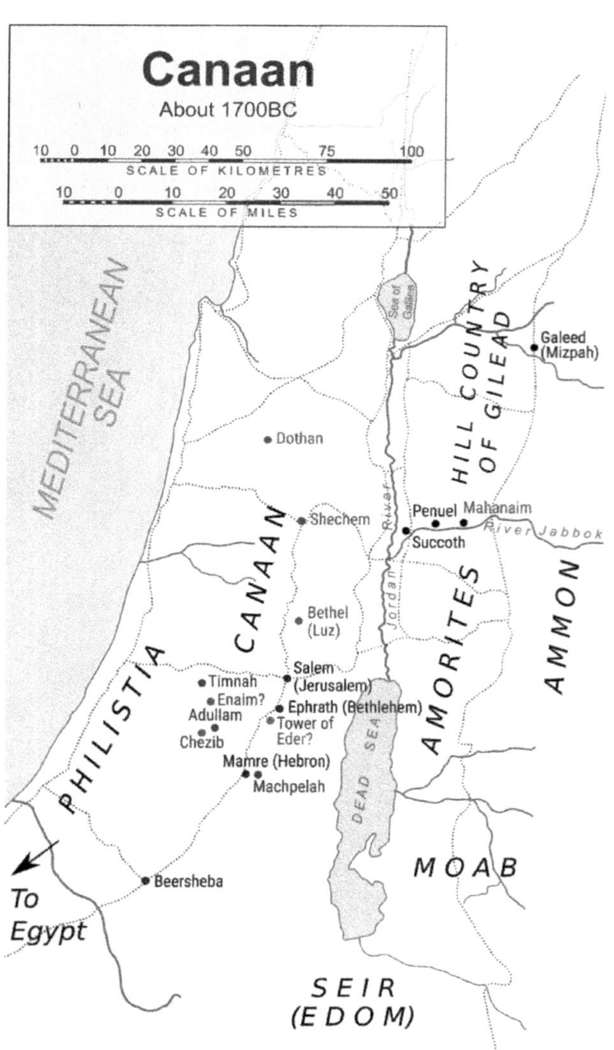

Canaan
About 1700BC
10 0 10 20 30 40 50 75 100
SCALE OF KILOMETRES
10 0 10 20 30 40 50
SCALE OF MILES
MEDITERRANEAN SEA
Sea of Galilee
HILL COUNTRY OF GILEAD
Galeed (Mizpah)
Dothan
River Jordan
Shechem
Penuel
Mahanaim
River Jabbok
Succoth
CANAAN
Bethel (Luz)
AMORITES
AMMON
Salem (Jerusalem)
Timnah
Enaim?
Ephrath (Bethlehem)
Adullam
Tower of Eder?
Chezib
Mamre (Hebron)
Machpelah
DEAD SEA
PHILISTIA
MOAB
Beersheba
To Egypt
SEIR (EDOM)

Chapter 5

Uncle Esau

Jacob was a twin. It would be hard to imagine two brothers more different than Esau and Jacob, but to find such differences in twins was even more startling.

Whereas Jacob was quiet, even to the point of timidity at times, Esau his twin was brash and confident, with a commanding physical presence – and that startling red hair that seemed to sprout from all over. His bushy beard jutted out and he always stood with his feet widely spaced, as if he felt the need to claim more space in the world than it wanted to offer him. For the rest, he had a thick shock of hair, bushy eyebrows, massive hairy arms, and a deep, powerful voice.

Esau strode through the world as if it were his, and as if all the people he met were his subjects. By contrast, Jacob was sensitive to the feelings of others, humble by both nature and practice – although that didn't mean he didn't do his best to get his own way at times. But he did try to avoid confrontation, which sometimes twisted his determination into deceit. It was this attitude that had caused such trouble between the brothers – that, and the fact that Esau's self-confidence meant that he rarely listened to anyone else.

Twenty years of absence must surely have made Esau's heart fonder toward Jacob? Jacob had no doubt that Esau would have killed him without compunction if he had had the opportunity twenty years ago. But family was family and he should reconnect with them if he could. The sparse family news he had received during that time suggested that Esau had got over his hatred of Jacob now that he had won land and riches for himself down south in Seir. Jacob certainly hoped so. Now that he had escaped from Laban and drawn a line between them, maybe he could do the same with Esau – though hopefully in a more friendly spirit.

As he was pondering what he should do, another of the strange events that had punctuated his life since the day he left his parents' tents took place. In Bethel, twenty years before, he had seen in his dreams angels going up and down a ladder, and had been sure that it must be the very house of God, the place in which God's heaven communicated with earth. Then, just a few months ago in Paddan-aram, he had seen a lone angel in a dream who had reminded him of his vow and told him to return to the land of his family. In meditating on that dream, he had come to some understanding of El Shaddai as a God who focused on the land he had promised to Abraham, but could send his angels even to faraway lands. Possibly there were special angels who worked alone in such distant places, keeping an eye on events that were happening so far from the centre of the world. It was hard to visualise how El Shaddai, the mighty one, might control and maintain his world.

Now he was back at the gates of the promised land, and once again he saw several angels together. Were God's angels concentrated in this region too? He felt that this was a camp of angels and wondered if the angel he had seen in Mesopotamia had been dispatched to him from this, God's camp. Jacob called the place "The Camp of God" and decided to stay in the area while he sorted out his family matters. He would feel safer with the angels of El Shaddai close by.

He sent a message to Esau suggesting a meeting. It seemed like a good idea, but when the messengers returned after finding Esau, they brought unexpected and frightening news.

Not only was Esau willing to meet Jacob, he was so eager to do so that he was coming immediately – with four hundred men.

"Four hundred men?" said Jacob to the messenger, in shock. "It doesn't take four hundred men to say 'Hello' to your twin!"

"No, sir," agreed the messenger. "He is a very powerful man now, sir."

"How soon will he be here?" inquired Jacob, looking around at the camp spread out tranquilly before him.

"In a day or two, sir."

"A day or two? But why would he do that?" asked Jacob.

"Well, actually, he plans to be here tomorrow, sir."

"Tomorrow? But… what…. Is he coming to kill us all?" Jacob was obviously remembering Esau's fury of long ago, sparked by Jacob's tricking of Isaac to gain the special promises reserved for the firstborn. He had seen the promise of death in Esau's eyes and couldn't forget it.

"He didn't seem unhappy to see us when we met him, sir," said the messenger. "In fact, he sounded quite pleased to hear that you were back."

Jacob waved his hands dismissively as if he couldn't believe the statement and looked around again uncertainly.

"He *must* be planning to attack… but maybe you are right. Oh, what shall I do?" Jacob wrung his hands, his forehead creased with worry.

His uncertainty lasted for the best part of an hour, but by the end of that time, he had decided what to do. He must divide the camp and separate the two halves. Then if one half was attacked by Esau, the other half might have a chance of escaping his violence. Quickly Jacob put his plan into action. After all, if Esau was planning retribution, he might attack during the night as they lay unsuspecting in their tents.

At first the servants and the family did not take the threat seriously, but fear is a powerful force and it was obvious that Jacob was genuinely afraid. Soon the packing up became urgent, and within two hours, half of the family had packed up and begun to move into another valley where they would not be visible from the road by which Esau would approach. In this group, carefully hidden from Esau's approach, were Rachel and Joseph and Leah and her children.

Then Jacob prayed. His prayer was an urgent request for help from the God of his fathers. Jacob's prayers were often negotiations with God – describing his situation and the ways in which God was responsible for the problems, or offering a commitment on the condition that God would do something for him. He struggled with God in prayer. This prayer was no exception, but it also included an honest acknowledgement of Jacob's need for God's help. He feared Esau and poured out his fears to God.

Darkness fell, and still Jacob was searching for a way out of his problems. No foolproof plan came to his struggling mind, but he did come up with an idea that just might help. Esau had always been a little obsessive about goods and power, so maybe if Jacob sent him a present his anger might be appeased…. The details of the idea gradually filled out in Jacob's mind, becoming more and more grandiose. Female goats, male goats, female sheep, male sheep, camels and their calves, cows and bulls, female donkeys and male donkeys. Each of these in a batch separated from all the rest so that Esau would come to group after group of animals as he approached. Hundreds of animals and lots of servants – not as a threat, but as a sign of good will, not to mention wealth and generosity.

The idea would also ensure that there were many people and animals between him and Esau. That would delay Esau, and the servants could tell him that it was all a present for him from Jacob. Yes, that should do the trick. He called his servants and spelled out his plan to them. That night, the servants collected together all the parts of his generous present and set off towards Esau. They would spread out along the road and they travelled so that there were significant gaps between them. For these servants, the night would be long, with little opportunity for sleep as they protected their animals from any optimistic predators.

Careful preparations had been made, but still Jacob was not satisfied. Twenty years had not allayed his fears, and now the steps he had taken so far had not done so completely either. On this night, Jacob's faith had failed him, so he must make his own arrangements for his family's safety. He thought some more and decided to undo his plan of splitting the camp. Instead, he would send all the children back over the ford of the Jabbok, putting some extra distance between them and his terrifying brother. But then again, now that he had sent a present, maybe it was best to send the entire company back over the stream….

Jacob could not rest, and he continued to think and rethink his options until everyone in the camp was on edge. Late though it was, the children were roused and both groups were dispatched in the dark, back across the Jabbok, there to set up camp once more in the dead of night.

Attempts to find sleep began all over again, but not for Jacob. He remained on the near side of the Jabbok, sitting and watching – and worrying. Then, in the pale moonlight, he saw a man walking as if to pass him by, and hurried to intercept him. It was almost unreal as they came together without words and Jacob put out his hands to stop the man. The man reached out to brush them aside, but Jacob grasped at him. He was astonished at the strength he felt in those hands and realised with alarm that if he was to protect his family, he would have to fight, with no guarantee of success.

Jacob was wiry and tough. Years spent in the fields, guiding and protecting the flocks, had toughened him both physically and mentally – as long as he didn't have too much time to think about what was happening!

Soon the two men were struggling with each other, one seeking to go past and cross the ford, while the other strove to stop him. As each grappled for a decisive hold on the other, occasional grunts of sudden effort escaped their lips. Sinews were stretched taut as bowstrings, and muscles exerted all the force that could be mustered. And yet, the struggle was not a fight to kill. Astonishingly, neither party tried to strike the other or to shed blood. It was disciplined wrestling – a striving for mastery through skill, strength and endurance.

The night was only half gone when the struggle began, but the time flowed past as it continued and the moon traversed the sky. As dawn began to lighten the sky, both of the combatants redoubled their efforts, the one to escape before sun-up and the other to prevent that escape.

Morning was breaking, light was spreading across the sky and flooding the landscape, yet still the man could not escape. His touch on Jacob's hip seemed innocuous enough, but it had an immediate result. Jacob knew a sudden excruciating pain and could no longer move his leg freely. But tenacity was baked into Jacob, and even then, giving up never occurred to him. He would not let the man go, and finally the first words of the encounter were spoken.

"Let me go," panted the man. "The day has broken."

Determined, but painfully injured, Jacob refused. The man's ability to inflict sudden damage with so little effort had warned Jacob that this was no ordinary man, and even made him wonder if this might be another angel of God.

"I will not let you go unless you bless me," Jacob insisted, hanging on tightly despite the pain.

"What is your name?" came the question, spoken in a strained voice.

"Jacob," he answered.

"You will no longer be called Jacob, but 'Israel', for you have struggled with God and with men, and have prevailed."

Jacob wondered if having his name changed really counted as a blessing. Abraham and Sarah's names had been changed by God and his new name spoke of contending with God, so this *must* be an angel. He asked, "Please tell me your name."

The man refused, yet gave Jacob other blessings before the two of them parted in the cool of early morning, Jacob limping because of his damaged hip. The day had barely begun, but already Jacob was exhausted, and the day couldn't be expected to get any easier. Esau was coming and no-one could predict what his attitude to his estranged brother would be.

With difficulty, Jacob crossed the Jabbok River once more and limped to greet his family. In the bustle of the camp, few noticed his limp, but Joseph did, and asked what had caused it. Jacob told the story and Joseph listened round-eyed to the exciting tale, marvelling at the idea that his father had seen the face of God in an angel while he himself had been sleeping! If only he could have been with his father when it happened, mused Joseph. His father had seen angels several times, and heard God speak to him too. Would he, Joseph, ever have the same sort of experience? He hoped so.

Once the tale was told, Jacob remembered his concerns and took Joseph with him to climb all the way to the top of the hill that edged the valley and see if there were any signs of Esau and his men.

Slowly they climbed together. Joseph helped where he could, but he was too small to be very useful. As they approached the summit, they turned and looked southwest. Esau would approach from there, and the hill was high enough that they should be able to see him well before he arrived. The sun had risen and presumably Esau and his men would be marching already.

It was Joseph's young eyes that saw a small cloud of dust rising in the expected quarter.

"Look, Daddy," he said, excitedly, pointing to the telltale cloud, "that must be Uncle Esau and his men."

"Where?" asked Jacob. His eyes were not so good, and that morning they were very tired.

Joseph pointed and finally managed to show his father where he was looking.

"Y-e-s," said Jacob, slowly. "I think you're right." He measured the distance with his eyes and then spoke more quickly. "We don't have very long to organise things. Let's go down."

Slowly, carefully, they descended the hill and made their way back to the camp. As they walked, Jacob tried to explain to Joseph what his plans were, reflecting as he did so that yet again he was treating Joseph as much older than he really was. He often found himself explaining things to Joseph that he wouldn't have even tried to explain to Reuben. Joseph always listened so carefully and seemed to understand so much.

On this occasion, Joseph had no difficulty understanding his father's plans, but the reasoning and the cause of Jacob's fear of Esau, these he found harder to understand. He would have liked to walk with his father at the very front, but instead, he would be at the tail end of the procession with his mother, both receiving the special care due to favourites.

Zilpah and Bilhah, the wives who had been Leah's and Rachel's maids – and who still could not command the same respect as the two sisters – they would lead the way with their children, Gad and Asher, Dan and Naphtali. Jacob reasoned that if Esau rediscovered his anger when he saw Joseph's wives or offspring, these could be sacrificed as the least valuable. After all, they were really only servant girls, despite their double duty as surrogate mothers. Each had borne him two sons at the behest of their mistresses, but that phase of life was over. Eleven sons was quite enough, particularly now that he had Joseph – that special, last son whom Jacob thought of as the son of his old age. What a wonderful son he was, both for his own sake and as the son of his beautiful Rachel! If only things had worked out better, with none of Laban's deceit that had weighed him down with three extra wives and all the complications that went along with that. How much easier life would have been if Rachel had been his first and only wife!

But no amount of pondering over might-have-beens would solve the immediate problem of Esau, and having some spare sons as a buffer to protect Joseph was a distinct advantage. Of course, he didn't want anything to happen to Dan and Naphtali or Gad and Asher, and he wished no harm to Bilhah or Zilpah either, but the fact remained that Rachel and Joseph were the centre of his life.

Yes, Leah would follow next with her children, and finally Rachel and Joseph would bring up the rear.

The decisions had been made and all that remained was to make sure that everyone knew their position. Then Jacob himself would set off to meet his brother, hoping that the presents which preceded him had placated Esau.

Long-nurtured fear can consume a lot of energy and planning – and lose many opportunities.

In the end, Esau wasn't angry at all. Instead, he ran to meet Jacob and welcomed him with open arms. The betrayal and deception were forgotten and Esau was glad to see his twin. He was not keen to accept Jacob's presents, but finally gave in to Jacob's repeated insistence. Then it was all over. Esau tried to arrange for Jacob to visit immediately, but Jacob was still cautious – engrained fear cannot be shaken off in an instant – and made his excuses. Esau left with his 400 men, feeling better about Jacob than he had done for more than twenty years.

Jacob was joyful, and the whole family felt as if a huge weight had been lifted off them. When Joseph thought back on those events over the next few years, what struck him most was the overwhelming fear that had filled his father, almost paralysing him. Still later, when Joseph himself had great reason to fear and long hours with nothing to do but think, he remembered again. From the time Jacob first planned to leave Haran until they finally settled down in Hebron[5], everything he did was affected by his fear: fear of Laban, fear of Esau, fear of neighbours and fear of death.

Joseph resolved to live with the fear of only one being: God. Known as El Shaddai, he was the mighty one of Abraham, Isaac and Jacob, and he had promised to care for Abraham and his descendants. Joseph was determined: fear of mankind should never be allowed to degrade his trust in God.

---

[5] Genesis 37:14

Chapter 6

A house in Succoth

Esau returned to his home in Seir and Jacob stayed behind, wondering what he should do next. After all, his excuses to Esau about not wanting to hurry the flocks were quite true.

After their urgent rush from Paddan-aram with its ill-tempered finale in the hills of Gilead, the pace of Jacob's party had slackened. In fact, it had been two full weeks before they had moved on from the heap of stones the disputants had built. Laban had named the heap "Jegar-sahadutha", its name an outpost of wordy Aramaic on the borders of the land promised to Abraham. Jacob had used the same name, "heap of witness", but had expressed it in concise Hebrew as "Galeed".

After that two weeks of rest and calm reflection, Jacob had slowly moved further south.

By the time the twins had met, many in Jacob's flocks had been heavy with young, and the first few lambs had already arrived.[6] The rest would come very soon – and the young of the other livestock too. Once the twins parted, Jacob led his family some distance up the River

---

[6] Most breeds of sheep are more likely to become pregnant as days become shorter which in Israel means the period July and August or later. Sheep have a gestation period of about 5 months.

Jabbok at a leisurely pace and then set up camp. This would be a good place for them to stay.

One afternoon as Jacob walked beside the River Jabbok, enjoying the warmth of the autumn sun, he considered his options. Maybe it was time to settle down: to build a house for the family, and sheds for the flocks. Jacob was in his late nineties; glad to be away from his father-in-law at last and determined to establish himself by himself. He refused to return tamely to his father, and could not even begin to contemplate joining his brother in Seir. Canaan was the land God had promised Grandpa Abraham.

As he mulled over the idea of settling down, he began to see other advantages in it. If he went to his father immediately, he had no doubt that he would be invited – ordered? – to rejoin his father's encampment, and he felt that doing so would be likely to cause major problems. His flocks were large, and trying to support them along with those of his father could easily cause the same tension that he had heard about between Grandpa Abraham and Uncle Lot: two large flocks cared for by herdsmen with conflicting loyalties. Remaining on the eastern side of the Jordan River – for some time at least – would avoid those problems.

He also wanted to make it clear that he was no longer just "stay-at-home-Jacob", the mother's boy who stayed with the tents. Jacob wanted his own position in the world, and that desire had been one of the driving forces in his stand against Laban. Throwing away what he had gained would be foolish. No, his family must be separate from his father – just as Isaac's own family had been, and now Esau's was as well.

He saw that building a house would provide a good reason for remaining separate from his father's encampment and make it easier to take a stand against going back "home" again.

This would be a good place to settle down – away from the jungles around the Jordan where lions and bears were far too common. Even so, some more permanent protection for the sheep and goats would be wise. Some people already lived in the area, but there was no problem with space. Jacob was welcome to stay, they said, even with his large flocks. In fact, they seemed quite keen on the idea of turning their scattered "village" into a town – as long as someone else would show the initiative needed to get things started.

As Jacob pondered his plan, he saw more and more advantages, not the least of which was comfort: avoiding the searing heat and freezing cold that were so typical of life in tents. Abraham and Isaac had both lived in tents, their lifestyle separating them from the people of the land. Abraham had always been friendly with some of the locals, but he had also kept them at arm's length by never moving into a town with its civic engagement and cultural integration.

Jacob felt that he was getting older, and living in a town would be more relaxing, avoiding the constant need to sustain independence, provide security and maintain a viable water supply.

A town had some advantages after all.

Jacob sat down on a rock beside the river and watched the sun setting over the mountains of Canaan. Soon, he would have to visit his father Isaac – whose health had improved astonishingly during Jacob's twenty years of absence, except for his complete blindness – but it would be best to do some building work first. He picked up a flat stone and threw it parallel to the surface of the water, watching as it skipped lightly across the cool water before suddenly bouncing a little higher into the air off a small ripple and disappearing beneath the water.

It was a pleasant change to have a river to sit beside on sunny afternoons, and its relaxing gurgle made his meditation even more satisfying. But the shepherds would already be bringing the flocks back to their pens for the night – he must return to the camp.

Smiling to himself, he stood up and walked towards their camp. Tomorrow he would start the planning for building a house. Imagine that, a house for a descendant of Abraham!

☙

The plan had not gone well. It wasn't the house that was the problem, nor was it the sheds and booths for the animals. Those features were enjoyable; pleasant. No, it was really the town, and the people who lived in it.

A simple house had been built in stages, first with a roof of tent material supported by rafters and stone walls. That had kept the winter rains off and everyone had been pleased with walls that did not flap in the wind and even managed to hold in some warmth. The next spring and summer had seen the house improved with a thatched roof and better doors, and much stronger sheds built for the animals.

Jacob's sons had learned a lot about building, and helped a lot with carrying and holding too. As usual, Joseph was the most thoughtful helper – despite being the youngest of them all. He watched what was happening and was always ready with the correct tool or a steadying hand whenever necessary. He talked to his father regularly about what would be needed next or if there was anything he could do. Jacob's oldest sons were reaching the stage where they were gaining useful strength, but some were more interested in avoiding work than in helping, and keeping an eye on them could be a major task. Even when not trying to dodge toil, some of them were just not practical, while others preferred to try to help in other ways, like Simeon was eager to do with hunting. Although only twelve years old, he was already quite accurate with a bow and liked to work with the servants who caught the game the family ate from time to time.

But Joseph went one step further, because he talked to his mother as well, and coaxed out of her both the dreams that Jacob had for the house and the minor irritations of construction that frustrated him. Many were beyond his 7-year-old understanding, but others were within both his comprehension and his ability to help. His father had been pleased beyond words when Joseph had collected stones from the river, ones as large as his young arms could carry, and brought them to the house to be used for building an altar to God Almighty. They had built the altar together, satisfying Jacob's desire for a visible memorial to the God who had taken him safely to Mesopotamia and brought him back from there not only in safety but in great prosperity.[7]

As the house progressed, so the family developed. Being away from Laban was a help, and Jacob was content that his wives were becoming less on edge and less competitive as everyone grew more accustomed to the family having a more stable size. Eleven sons and one daughter seemed to be God's will for the family, and even Rachel had ceased to chafe at her position as the wife with only one son.

Jacob did the best he could to walk the tightrope of satisfying the demands of four wives, two of whom must be treated to some extent as servant girls, while also deserving each the special care of a wife. Rachel must be

---

[7] There is no record of such an altar being built by Jacob during his stay in Succoth, but he seems to have built altars in many of the places he stayed, so he may well have done so there.

acknowledged as having first place in his heart, while Leah warranted a special position as his first wife and the mother of seven of his children. He still had not decided whether living in a house was making family life harder or easier, because the construction of the house was not the only change that was happening.

☙

When Jacob had started building there had been no town at all, just some widely scattered huts, a vaguely defined yearning, and an empty area in which no-one lived, near the river. But by the time a house had been built with sheds for the animals and many rooms for wives, children and servants, Jacob's camp had become quite a settlement. Settlements first attract attention and then hangers-on. People who were unhappy in other towns, but not confident enough to live on their own, began to settle nearby. At first they lived in tents, then other houses were built. Within two and a half years of Jacob's arrival, Succoth had truly become a town, and in just another year, Jacob was looking to move on.

The truth was, Jacob and his family just didn't fit in.

Building a house had really been Jacob's attempt to settle down and fit in, the action of a man whose youth has passed, and with it his desire to be different from everyone else. But he *was* different – like it or not. He couldn't fit into the life of an "ordinary" town. Jacob lived a life that was centred on El Shaddai, the God of his fathers, and the petty attractions of a town could not meet his needs.

As the town grew, so did the quarrels, the problems with drunkenness, the petty thefts. Idols appeared beside the river and near roadways, and deferential references to them littered the speech of many. Graffiti defaced walls with unwelcome messages and prostitutes began to ply their trade in the town. The more Jacob saw what was happening, the more he was reminded of the tales of Sodom that he had heard from his father. His relative Lot, having moved into Sodom, had lived through its destruction, only just escaping with his life, but without his wife. Instead, he had two sons that he had fathered through his daughters in his drunken sorrow. Lot had lost almost everything he had lived for, and his daughters' immoral behaviour had showed how life in Sodom had affected them. Jacob was determined not to ignore the lessons of the past.

Once more, Jacob called a family meeting, and told them all what he had planned. By that stage, Reuben was sixteen years old and showing signs of enjoying the life of the town. Simeon, Levi and Judah were showing the same signs, although to a lesser extent, so Jacob was not particularly surprised by the rather negative responses of all four when he announced that they would be packing up and leaving. In his mind, their responses vindicated his decision. His only concern was that he might already have left it too late. Time alone could answer that question, but whatever the answer, he was determined that he would not live in a town again.

Joseph had sat and listened thoughtfully while all the others had talked. It still amazed Jacob how quick Joseph was to listen and learn. Though he was only ten, it was rare for him to say anything without his words showing signs of careful thought.

❦

Jacob had not fitted in, but despite that, he and his family were the foundation of the town. News of their imminent departure was received with dismay, and many expressed great sadness. People who had refused to listen to his advice or opinions regarding the running of the town were genuinely disturbed that his wisdom would no longer be available. Those who had laughed at his ideas about the moral boundaries that should encompass life complained that the town would be left without a moral rudder.

They left anyway.

Their buildings, in prime positions in the growing town, were sold to eager buyers and Jacob became even richer. Was this God's blessing for a brave decision well made? His wives weren't so sure about that, and they weren't all very eager to leave either.

The presence of four wives – four mothers – made this family more complex than most. Zilpah and Bilhah were wives, but their status as wives was undermined by their original position as servant girls. Their marriages to Jacob had been a testament more to competition than to love. Jacob would always consider it his responsibility to care for them, and honour them for producing sons, but for them, the more intimate parts of marriage had lasted only as long as the fierce competition between Rachel and Leah had been displaying results. After the birth of Joseph, Jacob had begun to put his foot down. The competitive demands that had aimed to win his favour by producing offspring at almost any cost were refused, even from his beloved Rachel.

Zilpah and Bilhah had never been loved, and now they were not even needed. Jacob felt a little sorry for them, but they would have to be content with the protection and care that he could offer them.

And Leah? Jacob was very sorry for Leah. He could not love her, not as he loved Rachel, but he had begun to feel closer to her over the years, and she did work hard to keep the family together. Her children were closer to Jacob's ideal than the sons of Zilpah and Bilhah, but none of them could begin to compare with Joseph. If you had forced Jacob to talk about it, he would have admitted that mothers were not the only ones who had an impact on the way their children turned out, but he was completely convinced that Rachel could take a large part of the credit for how well Joseph was turning out.

Jacob went ahead of the party to choose a new place to stay. But this time they would not build a house. A temporary resident should not seek to put down permanent roots. God had promised the land to Abraham, but the time had not yet come for the family to inherit it. God had spoken about a period of 400 years during which the sins of the Amorites would continue to increase before God finally gave the land to Abraham's descendants. Until then, living in tents in a land owned and controlled by foreigners was best for the people of Israel. In his own mind, Jacob tentatively used the name that the angel had given him and thought about its double meaning. He *had* fought with God at times, opposed his plans and even broken his rules – and had normally ended up paying for it. But God had also fought for him and protected him when he needed protection.

For the moment, Jacob was willing to trust God and rely on his care as he looked for another place to live.

Chapter 7

Shechem

Jacob had heard of a place that he thought would be suitable. He led them down the Jabbok River to where it joined the Jordan River. They crossed the Jordan and then it was steep work, climbing up out of the rift valley and on into the high country beyond. There, in a valley between two mountains, Mount Ebal to the north and Mount Gerizim to the south, they saw in the distance a small town called Shechem.[8]

Some distance away from the town, they found a place to camp that was obviously not used for anything very often. A delightful spreading terebinth tree shaded the spot and gave a sense of comfort and permanence. Since the land around wasn't crowded, it wouldn't matter for a while, and there were enough of them that no-one was likely to come and evict them with violence anyway. Tents were set up first, then simple enclosures for the flocks and herds were built over the next few days.

Now, finally, after 24 long years, Jacob was really back, living in the land of Canaan. It was about 180 years since his grandfather Abraham had first moved to the land of Canaan. Abraham had lived and died in the land, his son Isaac had lived there all of his life, and now

---

[8] Genesis 33:18

Jacob himself had returned – yet still, the only property that any of them had ever owned was the plot of land with a cave that Abraham had bought to bury Sarah in. That burial cave had been used on two other occasions since: Abraham himself was buried there with Sarah, and Isaac had sadly buried Rebecca there. Jacob's blessing from Isaac had been won at a high cost: his farewell to his mother when he left on the long journey to Mesopotamia had been a final farewell. Although, at the time, Isaac's death had been thought imminent, instead it was Rebecca, the pious, gentle mother Jacob had adored, who had been unable to greet him on his return. She had died while he had been building a family and accumulating livestock in far-off Haran, and he would never see her loving smile again. The news had come not long before Jacob had left Laban's household.

On the second day after their arrival, some shepherds approached, leading their sheep and goats to find pasture. With consummate skill, Jacob and his sons managed to keep their sheep and goats from mixing with the local flocks, and the passing shepherds noticed and were impressed.

They were eager to hear about the newcomers, and Jacob in turn was eager to learn about the town they could see in the distance. News was exchanged, and by the time the shepherds moved on again, quite a bit more was known about the town of Shechem and its people. Apparently the leader was a man called Hamor, and any negotiations about land or grazing rights would have to be conducted with him. Jacob resolved to go and see the man, but not too quickly.

❧

Jacob was happy to be away from Succoth with its loose morals and the incessant pressure to conform to societal mores. Some of his sons, on the other hand, were missing the "good life" they had enjoyed in Succoth, and were eager to visit the town they could see in the distance. Joseph seemed glad to be in the land that Jacob had told him about, the land promised to Great-grandfather Abraham, and he was eager to help when Jacob began to build another altar to El Shaddai.

Together, they built the altar and Jacob named it after the God he worshipped, having felt again the presence of El Shaddai in that place. The altar was called "El Elohe Israel" or "God, the God of Israel".[9]

Offerings were made by Jacob on the altar and he did his best to involve the whole family in this devotion to the God who had guided him safely to Mesopotamia and back again.

☙

After a few days, Jacob went to Shechem to see what could be done about making more permanent arrangements for their camp. He took young Joseph with him, and they walked towards the town in the early morning sunshine. It was a restful scene, with the town nestling between the two mountains.

"This is a nice looking valley, father," said Joseph.

"Yes, and it is fertile enough that we can grow the food we need while still having easy access to pasture for the livestock."

"Who owns this land?" It was rather a grown-up question for a ten-year-old.

"The land belongs to the town of Shechem, and so probably to the prince there, a man called Hamor."

---

[9] Genesis 33:20

"Were you the prince in Succoth, father?"

"I suppose I was to some extent," replied Jacob, smiling at the thought. "But Abraham's family is not in this land to take possession of it. God has promised that he will give the land to Grandfather Abraham, and so both Grandfather Abraham and Isaac my father were content to wait for God to give the land rather than taking it or even buying it for themselves. The only land either of them took possession of was the land near Hebron that Grandfather needed because death comes to all of us. It was not land to live on, but land to bury the dead out of sight."

"So are you going to take or buy any land here, father?"

"Take? No," his father responded. "But buy? Maybe. We shall see what happens in our negotiations with Hamor."

"Would Great-grandfather Abraham and your father think that it was a good idea to buy land here? After all, if God will give it to us sometime anyway, surely spending money to buy it is a waste."

"When it is your turn to run a family, Joseph, you will realise that sometimes it is best not to insist on your own way too often; to just give a little bit here and there. Your mothers grew accustomed to Succoth, where we owned a house, sheds, sheep pens, and even the whole town if we had wanted to insist on it. Now that we have left Succoth, they feel that we have no place to stay, no security, nowhere to belong. They feel a little lost."

"Do you feel like that, father?"

"No, my son," Jacob said with a slow smile, "but that is different. I grew up knowing that we are waiting for God to give us our own land, and although I suppose I was fighting against that in taking land and building a house in Succoth, I am now content again to wait for God.

However, your mothers grew up with land and houses and a permanent place to stay – security as most people see it."

Joseph nodded and responded, "I see. So if I trust El Shaddai, I don't need to worry about where I am or what I own?"

"Yes, my son, that is exactly what I mean," said Jacob, surprised once again by his young son's ability to organise his thoughts into simple words.

"But aren't we rich, father?"

"Yes, very rich, thanks to God's blessings – but riches can come and go very easily. A large herd of sheep can suddenly catch a disease that kills many of them; robbers can steal thousands of cows in a night, and a fire in a camp can destroy many valuable things in a very short time. I have been blessed, and I give God a tenth of everything I get, to say thank you, but if I lost it all tomorrow, my biggest concern would be for my wives and children, who would find the loss very worrying.

"God has gradually taught me to trust him, but I have been very slow to learn, always wanting to control matters myself. Yet God took Grandfather Laban's flocks and herds and gave them to me. As you know, that is how I became rich."

"Tell me the story again, father," begged Joseph.

Jacob looked at the distance that remained to Shechem and judged that there would just be time to tell the story before they arrived if he slowed down a touch and hurried the story a little.

It was a favourite family story: how Grandfather Laban had agreed to pay Jacob all the speckled and spotted sheep and goats – the ones that were less valuable. Grandfather Laban was proud of his flock and their evenness of colour: the whiteness of the sheep and the blackness of the goats. His flock was well-known to be the equal of any flock in all of Paddan-aram. Yet there were still a few messy, speckled animals that he only kept because he couldn't bear to think of giving them up, and because, despite their own ugliness, they would often have children with the beautiful even colour that was so desired by sheep and goat breeders.

Jacob always tried to tell the next part of the story with a smile, as if it were part of a game, but it had been no game at the time: that night, Laban had picked out the few spotted and speckled animals in his flocks and sent his sons to take them three days' journey away to a place where Jacob had never been! It was dishonest, it was cheating, and – unless he was telling the story – Jacob still pursed his lips in anger whenever he thought of it. For Laban to cheat him of his wages before he had even given him any was unconscionable conduct! Nowadays, though, time had smoothed the sharp edge of that pain, and after that initial angry reaction, he was able to relax, remembering that God had looked after him despite Laban's despicable behaviour.

Indeed, Jacob had no trouble smiling as he remembered what had happened next. Suddenly the flocks had started giving birth to speckled young, and after a short time, Laban had been screaming to change the parameters. But however he changed Jacob's wages, whatever peculiarities of colour or marking were to belong to Jacob, as soon as it was agreed upon, the flocks started giving birth to young with those markings. Ewes with a fleece of the most beautiful, even creaminess would give birth to dark lambs with small streaks of cream across their flanks – but only as long as Jacob's wages were to be all the lambs born with streaks. Nanny goats without the faintest hint of white marring the jet-black perfection of their coats would suddenly give birth to triplets, each with a large white spot – as long as Jacob was promised the kids with spots.

Jacob remembered that it had been wonderful to be on the receiving end of such blessings, but what if El Shaddai chose to work the other way? Flocks could come and go with equal ease. It was not the flocks or herds that mattered, but the faith in El Shaddai.

By the time Jacob finished the story, they were approaching the gates of Shechem with its single sentry. Courteously, Jacob asked the man where he could find Hamor the prince.

☙

"Greetings," said Jacob, when he was ushered into Hamor's presence. "I believe that you are Hamor, the prince of Shechem."

"True, I am," replied the man, smoothly, "and you must be Jacob the son of Isaac, son of the great man Abraham."

Jacob inclined his head in agreement and then got down to the business at hand. "I believe that you own the land on which we have been camping. I would like to buy it."

"I'm very willing to sell you the land, since I'm sure you will be realistic about the price," Hamor replied, with a persuasive smile, "but why not move right into the town and join us here? There is plenty of room within the walls, and a walled city is safer for a family these days, don't you think? There are too many wandering mercenaries around, and a good strong wall is the only way to sleep safely at night. Of course, if you want to, you could take a small landholding outside the wall as well – a good place to keep your livestock, with some servants to look after them. That's what I do. Live in the town with us and I'm sure we'll be able to use your wise leadership for everyone's benefit – including yours."

There it was again, the urging for Jacob to join what he liked to call "the establishment" – those few who controlled the existing order of things; the men wielding power.

Succoth had already taken him too close to joining their ranks and he wasn't going to dabble with that again. He wanted space and he wanted to wait for El Shaddai to give them the land that had been promised. He wouldn't take the land, nor would he slowly merge into the rest of the inhabitants – Abraham's seed lost and indistinguishable. That was not what El Shaddai had wanted.

However, he might need to purchase some land. Maybe that would smooth the way towards living near them without living among them.

"We are tent-dwellers, Hamor," responded Jacob firmly. "Tent-dwellers… and wanderers to some extent. El Shaddai, our God, promised Abraham and his descendants a land, and until we receive it, we will stay as tent-dwellers. We will not live in a town – but we would like to live near a town. I like the look of this area. Is it peaceful?"

"Peaceful? Yes," said Hamor proudly, "peaceful and quiet. That's the way we like it around here, and we've worked hard to achieve it. The neighbouring towns leave us alone, and we leave them alone, too, pretty much."

"Any disputes about land or feeding areas?" pursued Jacob. "Wells and water supplies? My father has had a few problems over the years with those endless arguments."

"Oh no," replied Hamor, waving his hand reassuringly, "nothing like that. We sorted all of that out years ago, and we like to leave each other to live as we choose. There's still plenty of room for all."

"We'd like to stay near the town," repeated Jacob. "Do you see any difficulties with that?"

"In Shechem," said Hamor, earnestly, "we like everyone to have a commitment to the community, so that they have a stake in the development of the area, both within the town and beyond."

Jacob smiled. He had heard many of these words before from "the establishment", but he knew that their meaning varied widely. "So what does that mean for us?" he asked patiently.

"We like people who live here to own land," said Hamor, a little awkwardly, "to show that they are invested in the overall capital of the community. We're a little chary of those who want to stay and enjoy the benefits without commitment. Shechem is a place of shared aims; shared goals."

Jacob wasn't really interested in the reasoning; all he needed to know was whether he would have to purchase land before they would let him stay in the area. If so, he would cooperate with their biases. After all, he had enough silver to buy whatever he wanted in this quiet area.

By the time Jacob left, Hamor had agreed to sell him the land on which they were camping. It had taken a great deal of skill and patient negotiation on Jacob's part to convince Hamor that a place to live within the town was not necessary.

The other matters he could safely ignore for the time being. There was no need to force immediate agreement on everything. Hamor's repeated expectation that he would take his place in the civil organisation of the town could be countered later with the growing demands of his large family, not to mention his expanding flocks and herds. In the meantime, "Later!" would be an acceptable answer.

As Jacob walked away from Shechem with Joseph, he was quite satisfied with the results of his visit. They had a place to stay and he had avoided commitments that he was not willing to make. Not only that, but it had only cost him 100 pieces of silver.

A stray thought flitted across his mind as he looked at the young lad walking companionably at his side: Joseph had come to see the purchase; maybe he could have the land as an inheritance. Jacob was taken by the idea and smiled to himself as they walked towards their camp.

Three years passed and still Jacob's camp remained outside Shechem. Hamor's periodic urging for them to move into the town and assimilate had been resisted successfully: the family continued to stay mostly separate from the life of the town and the other nation-towns around.

Times were good. Jacob's flocks and herds continued to expand and there was no shortage of work to keep the family busy – despite the growing number of servants that assisted.

Some of Jacob's sons had tried to develop friendships with other young men from the town, but the carefully chosen distance and the incessant work made it difficult. Jacob was not sorry.

Jacob's sons were growing up, and so was his daughter, Dinah.

These years had been a time of relative peace for the family, but trouble was just around the corner.

Chapter 8

Dinah

Dinah didn't make it home that night.

At first, everyone thought she was just a little late, then a lot late. Someone – no-one could quite remember who – suggested that maybe she had done a bit more than just visit the house of one of her friends. Anyway, nobody knew, so one of the servants was dispatched to find her.

At first, they weren't really worried. Not really. After all, nothing serious could go wrong with a young girl visiting her girl friends. Could it?

Still, she was late and something had to be done.

The servant returned with two companions – a young woman called Basemath and a girl, Judith, in her early teens – and a tale that took some time to unravel. He led them first to Leah, Dinah's mother.

It turned out that the young woman was actually the girl's mother, although she couldn't have been more than 25. The girl was one of Dinah's new friends. They both looked rather pleased, although the girl's attitude might have been slightly tinged with jealousy. It was hard to understand. Both were eager to spill the news.

"Such news we have to tell you!" announced the mother. "You'll be so pleased."

"He's so handsome," breathed the daughter.

"She's made such a conquest! He's the son of Hamor, the prince, you know."

"Who are you talking about?" asked Jacob, who had arrived just in time to hear the end of this gleeful statement.

"Why, Shechem, of course," said Basemath.

Jacob and Leah looked at each other; but both looked blank. "Can you start the story from the beginning?" asked Leah.

"You'll be so pleased," repeated Basemath.

"It was a bit underhanded, I think," said young Judith with a pout. "The sneaky little thing."

"But such a catch!" smiled Basemath. "And so masterful…"

"You were going to explain," begged Leah. "Please start at the start."

"Oh, but surely you must know something about it? Dinah wouldn't have gone out with the rest of the girls if she hadn't been looking for love. That's why they went out today. Young girls, looking for young men to marry. Trying to catch the best one they can. That's how it works around here. That's how I got my husband, back when I was about Dinah's age."

Jacob and Leah looked at each other again, and now they each saw concern in the other's eyes.

"Can you please explain what happened?" repeated Leah, desperately.

"Well, it's all very simple really," said Basemath, obviously disappointed and a little miffed that her good news had not been welcomed with the joy it deserved. "Dinah went out with Judith and her friends this afternoon. They did the ordinary sorts of things that girls do to attract a husband, and Shechem noticed Dinah joining in with the rest."

"He talked to her very nicely, all gentle and kind," said Judith, "but it was obvious from the start that he liked the look of her. They spent some time talking and then he asked her to come with him for a walk, just by themselves, you know. Well, she said that she had better not, that you wouldn't want her to. I thought she was just being coy, so I took her aside and told her that it would be alright and that Shechem was a good catch. She said she really shouldn't, but I think she was weakening. In the end it was taken out of her hands anyway. I'm sure she liked the look of him – he's very handsome. But while we were talking, some of the other girls had been joking with Shechem, and one of them suggested that he should just pick her up and carry her off. And that's sort of what he did. He came over and told her straight out that he loved her. He was obviously serious. Then he leaned over and whispered in her ear. She looked pleased, but a little shocked, and then suddenly he just swept her up in his arms and walked out!"

Watching Leah's face, Basemath could tell that she was shocked by the news, so she hurriedly interrupted Judith, who seemed about to go into more detail. "Anyway," she said, "Shechem is just wildly in love with your daughter, and I'm sure you will hear from his father very soon."

Judith was obviously rather disappointed at this sudden truncation of her exciting story, and looked at her mother with irritation. But she took the chance to make one last contribution: "Apparently he carried her all the way to his room, up all of those stairs, too!"

Basemath hushed her daughter, and they left soon afterwards, hurrying to reach the town before the gates closed for the night.

As soon as they had gone, Jacob and Leah discussed the news. Leah was distraught. Jacob was deeply upset too, but unsure about what to do.

"Remember, Leah," said Jacob, doing his best to console her, "we can't be sure what has happened".

"Can't we?" sobbed Leah. "I don't think there's any doubt what has happened to Dinah."

"I suppose you're right, but we must go through and check. It is faintly possible that she hasn't been harmed."

"Is it?" asked Leah, still crying. She shook her head and wiped her tears. "I suppose it isn't completely impossible, but it's close. Oh, Dinah, Dinah – my dear little girl."

"They mentioned that this Shechem was a son of Hamor the prince, didn't they?"

"Yes," said Leah, dully.

"I suppose it must be the same Hamor from whom I bought this very piece of land that we are camping on," he mused. "What can we do to minimise the damage? I don't think we will be able to make his son suffer as I would dearly love to. Does this young prince think he can just grab any young girl who takes his fancy and carry her off? And it seems that the girls think it's a good idea too. What a society!"

The discussion went on for a long time as the two parents gradually came to terms with the devastating news. Retribution was high on their agenda, but they knew that they were hopelessly outnumbered by the people of the land, who saw nothing wrong with such behaviour. Besides, servants couldn't be relied on very much, and the sons who might have helped were away in the country, looking after the flocks.

If only Dinah had stayed home and not made friends with girls who had such different standards! But now it was too late. The damage was irreversible.

Nothing could be done that night. The city gates would be closed and would not be opened for anyone.

The long slow hours of uncertainty until the morning must be endured.

But still, it was conceivable that the story had not followed the path that seemed inevitable. It was possible, faintly possible…

Early the next morning, though, even that faint possibility was taken away.

News, particularly news like that, travels quickly – sometimes almost unbelievably quickly. The older sons of Jacob came with the flocks in the grey of dawn. They had heard the news and were seething with anger over their sister's treatment.

Jacob spent a while trying to calm them down a little. Some of them, Simeon and Levi in particular, were eager to attack the city as soon as the gates opened and kill everybody there. But Jacob felt that a little more caution was required, although he was pleased to see their fury at such an outrageous piece of presumptuous immorality.

Hamor and Shechem came to visit shortly after the city gates opened, by which time Jacob had calmed his sons down a little. However, their anger had not gone; instead, it had become a coldly calculating fury that would not rest until the wrongdoing had been punished. In fact, Simeon and Levi had still been so angry that Jacob had sent them away to do a small job together to take their minds off their rage.

Hamor came in and greeted them all happily, eager to have them agree to his plan to give their daughter to his besotted son and become fully integrated into the local community. Daughters could be swapped as wives and open trade enjoyed by all. Shechem didn't contribute much to the conversation, except to say that he was willing to give any bride price to get Dinah as his wife.

Of course, Hamor and Shechem hadn't brought Dinah with them – she had been left in the city.

Bargaining chips are valuable and possession is power.

Together, Jacob and his sons spoke politely to Hamor, discussing his proposals for friendship and cooperation, without sounding eager, but without showing the fury they felt.

It was then that Simeon and Levi returned to join the conversation. They had used their time to great purpose, but not at all the purpose Jacob had intended. They had a plan.

Jacob explained to them the proposals and was surprised when they readily agreed with the suggestions, with just one proviso: all the men of the city must be circumcised. They spoke convincingly about the advantages to everyone of this course of action, and in the end it was agreed on as the way forward.

Hamor and Shechem left to convince their fellow citizens that having Jacob and his family join the community would be worth the discomfort of circumcision. Apparently, they were successful: the family heard the news – and the complaints about the pain – before the end of the day.

℞

Two days later, Simeon and Levi put the main component of their plan into effect. Armed with swords and accompanied by some of the servants, they went into the city and killed Shechem, Hamor and all the other men in the city.

They also took away the wealth of the town and the flocks and herds belonging to those they had killed. They would never have killed any of the men just to take their goods, but once the owners were dead in payment for Shechem's offence, it seemed fair enough to claim the booty. That was simple, but what should they do with the surviving women and children? They had been angry and vengeful enough to kill every last man, but they had not been willing to kill the women and children. But now, what should they do with them?

"Maybe it would be easier to kill them," observed Levi, sardonically.

"It probably would be, but you know we couldn't do that," replied Simeon.

"So what do we do?"

"I suppose we'll have to take them back to the camp. We can't really leave them here unprotected, or someone will be sure to come along and abuse them or take them away as slaves."

"More people in the camp? We already have enough servants in the camp and the family isn't small either."

"Do you have any better idea?"

Levi didn't, so they rounded up the women and children and took them back to the camp.

Overall, the pair was pleased with the outcome: Dinah had been rescued and punishment had been meted out. Nothing could remove the fact that Shechem had humbled her, but Simeon and Levi were content that his immoral behaviour had earned its just reward.

Jacob, however, was not pleased and spoke sternly to Simeon and Levi – but only about the danger in which their actions had placed the whole family. The surrounding villages, towns and cities could, he said, easily join together and attack the family.

His sons were not very concerned. They viewed their actions as necessary: should a man be allowed to treat their sister as a prostitute? Jacob understood their attitude, but he was seriously worried.

And what of Jacob's God? What would his response be to these events?

Chapter 9

Rachel and Joseph

They were moving. After the horrible incident with Shechem and Dinah, God said to Jacob, "Go to Bethel and live there. Make an altar there to the God who appeared to you when you fled from your brother Esau."

El Shaddai's reminder, however, struck Jacob forcibly and he decided that he needed to purify the entire camp. He knew that some of his servants carried small idols around with them – mostly just as good luck charms, really – but he did not want any of these in the place that was the house of God. Also, the women and children from Shechem who had joined the camp had brought many idols from the ruins of their town. Presumably, too, none of them knew much about El Shaddai, and Jacob felt that they needed to hear about him.

So Jacob called everyone together and informed them of his plans. He told them about Bethel, explaining what the name meant and how he had given the place that name more than 30 years earlier when passing through on his way to Haran. "Since this place where we are going is dedicated to El Shaddai, God Almighty," he continued, "I don't want us to take any foreign gods there, so all of you need to get rid of any foreign gods you have with you. Idols of any gods, big or small, wood or stone or metal, whatever they are, bring them all to me and I will dispose of them here. El Shaddai is powerful – and none of us should be worshipping any other gods anyway. Other gods are just wood or stone, but El Shaddai is a living God who blesses those who serve him. Bring them to me before we leave tomorrow."

The pleasant spot where they had camped was dominated by a large terebinth whose shade formed a refuge of cool beauty. The children had spent countless hours exploring its thick canopy and many a peaceful family gathering had been held beneath its branches.

Jacob ordered a servant to dig a hole near the base of the tree, and soon idols were being placed in the hole. Many were wrapped in cloth, perhaps because their owners were not willing to completely sever all ties with their private deities, and hoped to return at some time to collect them.

Of the idols that were not covered, most were of little intrinsic value. Carved stone or wooden idols were included, but more valuable ones were conspicuously absent. Joseph, now 13 years old and almost as tall as his mother, noticed this and asked his mother about it. He was suspicious and wanted to know if his suspicions were correct. "Why are people only disposing of idols that are made of cheap materials, Mother? Are they just trying to look good to Dad? Will they just carve more as soon as we leave?"

"Well, I can't be sure what people intend," replied his mother, "but I don't think that is the reason."

"Then why?" asked Joseph.

"I think it's mostly that people find it easier to get rid of an idol that has little material value than to get rid of an idol made of something valuable like gold or silver or a carved precious stone. Often when people think of El Shaddai and the wonderful stories they have heard about him, they want to do something to please him. Imagine you had a large golden idol and a small carved wooden idol. You want to please God, so which idol would you get rid of?"

"I would get rid of both!" said Joseph decidedly.

Rachel laughed gaily at this unexpected answer and asked, "Why, Joseph?"

"I don't like idols, Mother. I like El Shaddai and I like the idea that there is only one God. You know how you have told me about creation and about the flood? Those are things done by just one God, where no-one could ask and no-one could argue. He doesn't need any help from anyone and no-one can stop him from doing whatever he wants. That sounds like a good God to me."

"You think that only a good God would send a flood to kill everyone?"

"That's not what I meant, Mother. The way he has treated our family shows me that he is a good God, but what I meant was that it sounds good to me, and it makes sense that El Shaddai is the only living God and that all of the other gods are just lumps of metal or wood or stone. I really can't see why people want them."

"People don't always have idols because they want to worship them. Sometimes people keep more valuable idols just because they are valuable. Gold and silver idols can always be traded for money, food or goods."

"But if you don't worship the god, why have it? Surely if you just want gold you can keep it as gold?"

"Two reasons, my dear. Sometimes people are superstitious and would not steal a god, though they might steal a lump of gold. And sometimes, people have the god mostly as gold, but with a little bit of a wish to have a god too. Not seriously, but just a bit."

"I can't see why anyone would do that. If you believe in a god, surely you must believe in it completely or it's not really a god?"

"That makes sense if you understand what a god is. But many people use gods as something to hang on to and admire, not to be bossed around by. I have felt like that at times, Joseph."

"Really, Mother? You never told me that before."

"No – I'm not proud of it, dear."

"I can't imagine feeling like that at all, Mother. I am sure of my God and sure that he can demand obedience from me because he has created me and knows what is best."

"Yes, you know that, and it is what your father and I have tried to teach you. But when I was your age, I didn't feel like that. I wanted money and comfort, but I wasn't completely happy with having no idols at all. I suppose that I mostly learned it from my father. You remember what Grandpa was like, don't you?"

"Yes, a little," said Joseph.

"Well, Grandpa was always wanting money, and he would do almost anything to get it. I don't want you to think too badly of him, but he was always willing to treat people badly if he thought he could get more money that way. You know how Dad ended up with two wives, don't you?"

"Yes, I think so," said Joseph carefully. It was a subject that was never spoken about in public, but the brothers had heard odd details from time to time through the servants and had tried to put all of the pieces together.

"You know that Dad wanted to marry me?"

"Yes."

"And you know that Dad agreed to work for seven years so that he could marry me?"

"Yes."

"Well, Grandpa tricked Dad so that he could get seven extra years' work from him. Did you know that?"

"I thought it was because Mother-Leah was older than you."

"That was what Grandpa said, but the real reason was that his trickery got seven more years' work out of Dad. Your father is a very good shepherd and Grandpa saw that the sheep and goats did very well under Dad's care, so he decided that 14 years of that sort of success would make him a rich man. And it did. What Grandpa didn't realise, and I suppose I didn't realise either, was that the reason Dad did so well was that he worshipped El Shaddai faithfully."

"But if Grandpa just wanted money, why was he so upset when his household gods disappeared?"

"Well, that was what I meant about not being able to let go of a god completely. Grandpa still wanted an idol as a sort of good luck charm, and also as a way of storing money. His household gods were made of gold, my dear. Solid, heavy gold. They were worth a lot of money, and Grandpa hoped that they would also bring him luck because he was acknowledging one of the gods. I understood how he felt because that was how I used to feel too, before I married Dad. And I still felt like that at times when things didn't go well."

"Is that why you stole Grandpa's household gods?"

"What do you mean?" Rachel looked at her son in shock.

"Did you take Grandpa's household gods because you wanted money and you thought you would miss them?"

"What makes you think I stole them, my dear?"

"When we were running away from Grandpa, you came hurrying out of the house carrying something and put it in a pocket on the camel's saddle. Then, when Grandpa caught up with us, I was with you in your tent when you were sitting on that saddle while he searched. I don't remember very much about it – I suppose that I was too young – but I remember guessing that you were hiding the household gods. I was so frightened because Dad had said that if anyone was found with the gods, they would be killed. I have never forgotten the fear I felt."

"Well, my dear, you were right. I took them. I shouldn't have done it, but I wanted to make Grandpa suffer and I wanted to have the security of some money. I also wanted to have the security of the family gods that we had always had while I was growing up. All of those reasons were bad, and even if my reasons had been good, the gods weren't mine to take anyway. It was terribly wrong and I have regretted it ever since – but not enough to do anything about it. I still have the gods. Maybe I still haven't really got over my desire to keep them."

"Then why don't you get rid of them now?"

"But Joseph, I don't want your father to know that I did it!"

"Maybe I can slip them into the pit when no-one is watching. We could wrap them up in a cloth – some other people have been doing that."

It was quite a reversal of roles – a parent being encouraged and guided by her child. Rachel smiled at the thought, but Joseph didn't notice. He was eager to get on with the job, to dispose of the stolen gods once and for all.

"Joseph, my dear, I'm sorry that I caused you such fear by my foolishness. And I'm sorry that you have had to live with the knowledge that I stole Grandpa's household gods. Parents are meant to set a good example to their children and I certainly haven't done so with this. Will you forgive me?"

Joseph looked a little shocked that he should be asked to forgive her. "Of course I forgive you, Mother. I know that you are sorry. You have been sorry for many years."

"I hope you will be a stronger person than I have been, my dear. Don't give in to temptation. Resist it even when it is hard, or when you are feeling angry or sorry for yourself. Your father has shown me how to grow in godliness, and I have much more faith in God now."

"Shall we wrap up the household gods now?" asked Joseph, persisting in his desire to take the final step to remove this temptation.

"Yes," she smiled. "I have kept them hidden under my bed ever since we arrived here. I'll get them." She went across to her bed and rummaged about underneath. Finally finding what she sought, she pulled it out. It was a cloth bag, and the way she lifted it showed that it was heavy. She brought it across to where Joseph was sitting and gave it to him. "You'd better take this and get rid of it now, before I change my mind."

Joseph took the bag and wrapped it tightly in another cloth, then picked it up and tried to make it look as if it didn't weigh very much at all. He walked out of the tent, crossed to the tree and put the bag into the hole. Nobody was there and he saw no-one nearby. Straightening up again, he walked back to the tent where his mother was waiting nervously.

She put her hand on his arm and said, "Oh, Joseph," then burst into tears.

Joseph didn't really know what to do, but he showed sympathy as much as he could, and after a while her sobbing quieted.

"You don't know how much those household gods have worried me ever since I took them – and now I am free, thanks to you. I never expected that my son would help me in learning godliness, but thank you."

⊂℞

There were never any questions asked about those gods, and the next morning, Jacob made one last call for anyone with foreign gods or items of false worship to dispose of. A few more idols were casually dropped – or carefully laid – in the pit. Some people even removed their earrings and added them, which Joseph found surprising. Obviously they considered their earrings to be some form of religious devotion. He didn't understand how, but he never asked because he didn't want to know.

The hole was filled in and pressed down, then the family set off for Bethel.

Chapter 10

Bethel

It was a subdued group of travellers that left behind their camp and the deserted town of Shechem, where Dinah had been abused and all the inhabitants annihilated. The memory was heavy for Jacob to carry, for it was the first time that true tragedy had struck his family. Jacob was also afraid. Many people had died, and surely some must have relatives and friends who lived in the areas around? What would happen if those relatives decided to take revenge? In Jacob's mind was the nagging fear that they might form an alliance and attack his family.

But his fear was without foundation – his God had everything under control. God never said whether Simeon and Levi had done right or wrong, but he did protect the family. As they travelled, God sent a terror upon the cities that were around them. Nobody attacked or pursued them as they left Shechem with its terrible memories, and that one plot of land that Jacob actually owned – purchased from a man now dead. The land, with its shady terebinth and its cache of useless gods, was left behind without a qualm as they travelled instead towards the house of God.

At that time, the town was called Luz by its inhabitants and the place where Jacob had slept and had his amazing vision was not within the walls, but in a small valley nearby. When they arrived at Luz, Jacob sought out the valley and found once again that hollow in its side – a comfortable place for a lone traveller to sleep for the night when the town gates were closed against him.[10]

He described to his family the visions that had filled his dreams that night and his sons listened spellbound to his tale of a ladder reaching from earth to heaven while angels climbed up and down it. Even for Rachel and Leah, the recounting seemed more real as they stood in the very hollow where Jacob's startling dream had shown him God at the top of the ladder and presented the voice of God extending to him the blessings promised to Abraham.

Over the years, the pillar he had set up to honour El Shaddai had fallen over – or been pushed – so he followed God's instructions and built a new altar.

He also gave the place another name, "El-bethel", meaning "the God of the House of God". This, he explained, was not merely an empty house, palace or temple – here was the living God himself.

As they stayed in the place, God spoke to him again, saying, "Your name is Jacob but you will no longer be called Jacob. Instead, you shall be called Israel." And God also said to him, "I am God Almighty: be fruitful and multiply. A nation and a company of nations shall come from you, and kings shall come from your own body. The land that I gave to Abraham and Isaac I will give to you, and I will give the land to your offspring after you."

---

[10] Genesis 28:11 tells us that Jacob arrived after sunset and Genesis 28:19 speaks of the place first being called Luz. This may mean that a town called Luz already existed in the place when Jacob first passed through, in which case its gates may have been closed, forcing Jacob to sleep nearby. Alternatively, a town called Luz may have been built there between his visits.

Then God went up from him and Jacob set up another pillar of stone there. He poured out a drink offering on it and poured oil on it.

Another tragedy struck while they were at Bethel: Deborah, Rebecca's old nurse, who had been with them for some years – since the first time Jacob had visited Isaac after their return from Haran – died. They buried her under an oak tree, a little further down the valley. She was very old by then, having travelled with Rebecca from Haran and having known Jacob all his life.

Chapter 11

Benjamin

The news came as a big surprise: Rachel was expecting another child! After more than twenty years of marriage with Jacob, twenty years during which only the beloved Joseph had come of their union, Rachel was to be a mother again.

Jacob was overjoyed and broke the news to Joseph with a wide smile and an extravagant hug. Joseph was happily excited and ran immediately to speak to his mother. He found her a little unsure: happy but concerned. Joseph's birth had been difficult and Rachel had fears that she couldn't really discuss with Joseph. He was, after all, only 14 years old, and there was much he could not yet understand about life, despite the ready sympathy he showed as he sensed her worry.

His brothers responded in various different ways, as people are wont to do. A few liked the sound of a new little brother in the family, but most would have been happier to accept a new camel in the family. A baby, particularly one who would be another of Jacob's favourites, was not an irresistible blessing!

The weeks passed, until one day Jacob decided that it was time to move again, away from Bethel – the house of God – to Hebron, where his father and grandfather had lived for so many years. Isaac was 165 years old by that time and once again in poor health. As when Jacob had gone to Haran, there were concerns that he was close to death, so the family packed up and moved.

Before the camp moved on, though, Jacob gave the women of Shechem a choice: any who wanted to come with the family of Israel as servants were welcome to do so, but any who preferred to leave could go free with their children wherever they wished. A few immediately sought refuge in the town of Luz, but most chose to stay, including Dinah's friend Judith and her mother Basemath. Although devastated by the slaughter of the men of Shechem, they had gradually come to accept – at least partly – that it was the immoral behaviour of the town that had triggered the disaster: not that the family tried to claim that the massacre had been truly justified. Over the months spent in the camp, they had seen that life within this family was generally much more satisfying and tranquil than the turbulent life they were accustomed to. The women and children of Shechem had often been beaten or abused by the men, and many of the "wives" had been abandoned for another woman more than once. Basemath suspected that in Luz, she would probably return to a life of insecurity and uncertainty. Life as a servant in this family was better than life as a wife in Shechem had been. She and Judith had also learned a little of the God of Jacob and begun to appreciate some of the benefits of his moral requirements.

As they left Bethel, Rachel was getting close to the time when her baby could be expected, but everyone was confident that they could make the two-day trip to Hebron before anything happened.

Unfortunately, they were wrong, and the events were tragic. Rachel went into labour a little before the family reached Bethlehem, and everyone stopped to wait for the birth before travelling on to Hebron. Labour was hard, and the delivery of a new baby boy was quickly followed by the death of his mother.

Knowing that death was approaching, Rachel had named her son "Ben-oni" – "the son of my sorrow".

Jacob was heartbroken, but the implications of the name his beloved Rachel had chosen were too upsetting to be borne, so he called the baby "Benjamin" instead. Joseph was devastated as his beloved mother was buried on the same day that his new baby brother was born.

Leah and Rachel had grown closer again over the years in Canaan as the competition of childbirth had gradually faded away. Leah mourned deeply over the death of her younger sister and took Benjamin as her special responsibility. A motherless child sparks sympathy in many hearts, and most of the women in the party did their best to help. A wet nurse was found and the tiny baby was fed and cared for.

The journey to Hebron was never completed. News came that Isaac was no longer at death's door, and Jacob was content to travel only a little further and camp near Bethlehem.

Joseph eagerly watched his little brother grow, and enjoyed his company as a reminder of their mother. Jacob also spent plenty of time with Benjamin, and maybe that helped the relationship between Jacob and Leah. No longer was there any competition; no longer was Leah spurned in preference to Rachel. Rather, Jacob appreciated the work Leah did in caring for the son of his favourite wife.

Sad though the event was, the results over the longer term were mostly advantageous in family life. Leah was open to positive spiritual leadership and, over time, she benefitted significantly from spending more time with Jacob. Jacob also found comfort in her gentle sympathy. The corrosive effects of competition were gone and young

Joseph spent much more time with Leah than he had done in the past. Children do not normally inspire improvements in the character of adults, but Joseph was an exception. Leah benefitted from increased contact with Joseph with his unflappable reliability, and over time those benefits slowly spread to at least some of her sons.

Those improvements, however, were in the longer term. In the short term, life for the family would be difficult.

Chapter 12

Beyond the tower

Jacob withdrew into himself for some time after Rachel's tragic death. He couldn't bring himself to travel far from the tomb of his lovely Rachel, and his sons felt the difference. Leah's sons had always known that their mother was only second best, but now, they found that Rachel kept the keys to their father's heart even in death, and Joseph took all the respect Jacob had to offer to his sons.

Judah responded particularly badly. He resented the treatment of his mother and began to look for opportunities to leave home. Home at that time was beyond the Tower of Eder that was near Bethlehem as you head south, but young Judah travelled much further afield, looking around for a home of his own.

In his travels, he struck up a friendship with an Adullamite called Hirah. Hirah had no real knowledge of El Shaddai, but at the time, Judah didn't care. He wanted to escape his family, and Hirah gave him just such an opportunity. While staying for a while with Hirah, he saw, and was immediately attracted to, a young woman who was the daughter of a Canaanite named Shua. He took her. Really, it wasn't much different from how Shechem had behaved with Dinah, but they were both satisfied, and her parents were glad to welcome him into their family.

Marriage suited Judah, and for a time he was glad to be away from his family. His wife presented him with three sons in quick succession and he felt little need for El Shaddai or the family's long-held belief in the land they had been promised. Life was good. Life was free of boundaries. Life could be whatever he made it.

Meanwhile, the rest of the family stayed together and endured the changes and sadness that Rachel's death had brought.

Rachel's maidservant Bilhah was left in a difficult position. She had no mistress either to serve or to protect her, but only a husband who had never wanted her as a wife and had long since ceased to notice her charms. Indeed, now he tried to avoid her completely because she reminded him of the beautiful woman whose bewitching smile he would never see again.

Reuben was a sensitive and kindly young man. He would never be single-minded or determined enough to achieve real success in life, but he felt the loneliness and insecurity of this youngish servant woman whose role in life was so utterly confused. She was mother to his younger half-brothers, but still young enough to tug at his heartstrings and more besides as he sympathised with her in her troubles.

Reuben's gentle sympathy led to a deepening friendship between them, and it was not long before the unequal friendship became more than it should have been.

The illicit relationship did not last long. Somehow, Jacob heard of it and called Reuben before him. It was an uncomfortable interview and Reuben was left in no doubt that his behaviour was completely unacceptable – outrageous, in fact – and had dishonoured his father. It was something that ought not to be done. Of course, Reuben knew that, when he thought about it, but he was too liable to act first and think later, to rush off in one direction and only see his folly later.

As he rebuked Reuben, Jacob couldn't help thinking of Joseph. A man couldn't have more than one firstborn son, could he? Yet Jacob felt that he had two or maybe even four – and he couldn't help seeing the contrast between Joseph and the others. He was confident that Joseph would never do anything like this.

He would have to think more about it, but maybe he should announce that Joseph was his firstborn, not Reuben. Reuben's behaviour needed some clear and unequivocal punishment.

"Your inheritance will be affected by this, Reuben," he concluded, and closed the interview.

Reuben might be profuse in his apologies, but Jacob wasn't particularly confident that he wouldn't do the same thing again if the situation arose once more.

Joseph was stable, solid as a rock. But Reuben – he vacillated like water swirling in a bowl. Young men sometimes change as they mature – and not always for the better – but Jacob was almost certain that Joseph would make a much better leader for the family than Reuben.

Chapter 13

Sixteen

Joseph was sixteen years old and had been growing quickly. No-one disputed the fact that he was now taller than most of his brothers, but then again, a few of them were still growing too. Nevertheless, he was significantly taller than diminutive Bilhah's two sons, Dan and Naphtali, while Zilpah's younger son, Asher, seemed to have stopped growing already, and was the shortest of them all. From a very young age, Joseph had been taller than Zebulun, his next older brother, and he had always revelled in the fact. Really, Judah and Issachar were the only two who were still thought by most to be taller, but Joseph was sure that he was actually taller than Issachar now. That left only Judah, and they didn't see him very often, busy as he was with his young family. Joseph hoped to pass him soon too. Everyone said it wasn't important, and Joseph knew they were right, but it would still be nice to be the tallest.

Jacob had reached one hundred and seven years of age and was beginning to shrink a little, as older people do. Although, of course, nobody knew it at the time, he had only forty years of life left, a significantly shorter life than that of his ancestors. Sadly, most of his remaining life would be spent without his favourite son, but nobody knew that either.

Isaac was one hundred and sixty seven years old, only eight years short of the ripe old age his father Abraham had achieved. Isaac's blindness made him dependent on others for many things, and the death of Rebecca had left him very lonely. Jacob had visited Isaac on several occasions since returning from Paddan-aram, but most of the time the two families had remained separate, spreading their extensive flocks and herds over the large areas they each needed. Isaac had found a place where arguments about water and pasture were minimal, and his servants maintained the flocks in the areas around Hebron and further south. Jacob's flocks and herds grazed in areas to the north, and he made sure that there was no overlap between the areas they frequented.

Early one morning, a party prepared to travel from Jacob's camp to Mamre, planning to visit the old man, who was ailing again.

Jacob led the group and Leah accompanied him. Reuben went as well, but that may have been because Jacob didn't feel that he could trust him enough to leave him in command of the camp. Joseph went too, partly because Jacob simply liked to have him around, and partly because he was proud of Rachel's older son, now so tall and with such a level, searching gaze. Naturally, Leah brought little Benjamin, and her two youngest sons Issachar and Zebulun rounded out the party. Quite a large company of servants also came to provide security and help with the menial tasks.

Simeon and Levi were to direct operations for those who stayed behind in the camp, and the rest of Jacob's sons would do their normal work of caring for the flocks. Jacob hoped that they would be diligent in that task; he had suspicions about their work ethic.

It was a typical sunny Canaan morning as the party set off. Flocks of birds were flying high overhead in the cloudless sky, and their plaintive cries could be faintly heard from time to time. Joseph was excited to be setting out on a journey, although it would not be a long one: they should arrive in Hebron before sunset. However, he was enjoying the change from the ordinary, humdrum routine of camp life. He was happy in the crisp morning air, happy to be with his father, and happy anticipating a meeting with his grandfather. Briefly, he wondered how his other grandfather, Laban, was – they never heard much news from him – and remembered that other exciting morning ten years before when they had left Paddan-aram in such hurried secrecy. He thought with regret of his mother too, and looked wistfully across at little Benjamin, who was riding with Leah on her camel just a little in front of Joseph, beating his heels against the camel's saddle and smiling happily.

In fact, everyone in the company seemed to be happy, all equally pleased with this variation in the normal repetitive cycle of everyday life. Only Jacob appeared to be thinking with concern about what might happen while they were away.

The day passed smoothly and quickly, and it was nearly sunset when they arrived at Isaac's camp near the oaks of Mamre. Isaac was sitting at the entrance of his tent, his blind eyes turned toward the approaching company.

"We're here, Father," called Jacob, knowing that the old man could not tell by sight who his visitors were, but would, of course, recognise his voice.

"Jacob, my son," replied Isaac in a quavering voice, "it is good to hear your voice again."

Jacob wondered if this was a reference to that day when he had tried to convince his father that he was Esau. In any case, it was safest not to reply. The party dismounted from their camels and Jacob walked to the tent doorway where his father sat, with Leah and the boys following.

"How are you, father? Are you happy here in Hebron?"

"I am content, Jacob, and my servants look after the flocks and herds very well. But it is good to have a visit from my family."

"Has Esau visited you recently?"

"No, not since you returned from Paddan-aram. It is probably better so. He is not interested in getting to know El Shaddai at all and cannot understand why I fear him."

"He never could, father. It was one of the reasons why we didn't get along very well, even before things went so badly wrong."

"You are right, but I hoped he would learn."

"Did he want to learn?"

"I'm not sure, but I am very pleased to hear your voice. I am still lonely without your mother and your voice reminds me of her."

"I understand what you mean, father. Joseph's voice reminds me of Rachel, too."

"The men of our family have had to get used to the early deaths of our wives," said Isaac sadly. "I still remember when my mother died; it was her death that made my father look for a wife for me. That was more than 100 years ago now, and God brought your mother Rebecca as a wife for me."

"I thought finding a wife would be as easy for me as it had been for you," said Jacob wryly, "but it didn't work out that way. Still, God has looked after me through all those troubles." He looked across at Leah, and their shared smile revealed a little of how much their relationship had improved since those early days of marriage.

"My getting a wife couldn't possibly have been any easier than it was. Indeed, God has looked after me throughout my life, and passed on his blessings to you."

Jacob wasn't quite sure how to respond. When it happened, Isaac hadn't been at all pleased that God's blessings had passed to Jacob. In those days he had always preferred outdoor Esau, revelling in the food his skilful hunting procured.

"Not so quick to reply this time, eh, Jacob?" asked Isaac after a short pause. His voice faltered a little with age, but a smile could still be heard.

"No, father, I'm not sure what to say. Are you content now with God's choice of who should receive the blessings?"

"Yes, I am. God got what he wanted – and so did you and Rebecca. 'Abraham, Isaac and Jacob' is how God has directed our family tree."

"True, father. When Grandfather Abraham died, you had two sons, but God only chose the younger. Grandfather never got to see any great increase in the family, did he, despite God's promises? He had only one chosen son, you; and you had only one chosen son. And at that time, I had none."

"But even so," said Isaac, "he didn't doubt that God would give him descendants as many as the stars of heaven. He was still confident, and now it has begun to be fulfilled through you."

"Yes, indeed. Twelve sons, and some of them with sons of their own now."

"Which ones have you brought with you?"

"Some oldest ones and some youngest ones." It was a game they always played at meetings like this – "guess the sons". Isaac was completely blind, and he didn't meet the boys often enough to learn their voices properly, so it was mostly a guessing game with Jacob giving hints.

"Reuben, Simeon, Levi?"

"Reuben and Joseph – each the oldest of their mother."

"Is that all the 'oldest' ones?"

"Of sons, yes. And Leah is here too."

"Welcome, Leah."

Leah greeted the old man and gave him a hug, saying, "I've brought you some special stew, father."

"Buttering me up, like Rebecca and that husband of yours did. What are you all trying to trick me into this time?" The old man's smile softened his harsh words, and his sightless eyes looked at her almost as if he could see her answering smile.

"Reuben and Joseph," said Isaac, "neither of you has said a word yet."

"Sorry Grandfather," said Reuben, standing in front of Isaac but making no move to greet him. "What would you like me to say?"

Joseph, meanwhile, took the old man's hand and said, "May God bless you, Grandfather. I have seen thousands of birds flying overhead today. Do you recognise them from their calls?"

Naturally, Isaac responded to Joseph's question rather than Reuben's, and for a few minutes the discussion focused on the bird and animal life that proliferated in the land they had been promised.

"I miss seeing all of the living creatures, and it has been so many years now since I could see properly. My father Abraham always looked forward to a time when El Shaddai would make us all young again, when all the niggling problems of old age will be taken away and we will have the land to live in forever. For me, sight is what

I want most. In the meantime, though, I need to try to work things out without it. Who else came with you, Jacob?"

"Leah's two youngest sons, father."

"Ah, greetings, Issachar and Zebulun." Isaac's age had not dimmed his memory or his sharp mind. The two came forward to greet their grandfather, and then Isaac asked Jacob, "Is that all the 'youngest' you were talking about?"

"Me, too," said a young child's voice from beside Leah where Benjamin had been standing, quietly watching proceedings.

"Little Ben," said Isaac, smiling again, using the pet name for Benjamin that seemed to come so easily from them all.

"Ben big boy!"

"A big boy now, are you? I can't see you though. Come and sit on my lap so that I can tell how big you are."

Joseph helped Benjamin onto Isaac's lap and the old man wrapped his arms around his youngest grandson. "You are getting bigger," he said.

"Grandpa see with hands?" asked the piping voice.

"No," said Jacob, "Grandpa can't see with his hands, but he can feel how big you are. When God fulfils his promises and gives us the land, then Grandpa will be able to see again. But not yet."

"And then our family will fill the land, won't we father?" asked Joseph.

"Yes, I suppose we will."

"When?" asked Reuben.

Isaac answered before Jacob could, "When I was younger than you, Reuben, God told my father Abraham to do a horrible thing. Of course, he never intended to let him finish the job, but my father didn't know that – and nor did I."

"Was that when God told him to kill you?" asked Issachar, eager to get as much of the story as they could.

"Yes, Issachar – that was your voice, wasn't it?" His identity was confirmed and then Isaac continued. "El Shaddai told my father to take me to the land of Moriah and offer me to him as a burnt offering. We set off early in the morning with two young servants and a donkey carrying a load of wood. Father didn't know the place where we were going so he couldn't be sure there would be wood available. He was always very thorough. And willing to obey. Well, he didn't tell me what was going to happen, and I'm very glad he didn't. I am still a bit terrified of God and it probably comes from that incident, even though God made sure I didn't get physically hurt at all.

"Anyway, I kept asking questions, and one of my father's answers seemed rather strange, but he was really predicting the future. He said that God would provide the lamb.

"When we arrived, an angel of God called to my father and told him not to kill me. God provided a lamb instead, and then he made more promises to my father, promises that talked about lots of descendants and about one special descendant who is probably to be a leader, but we really don't know much about him. The main point is that 'God will provide', and he will provide on that very mountain, which is well within the land that God has promised us. God will provide someone special in our family, and there will be some connection with that lamb, too. Maybe God will tell us more sometime before this descendant comes."

After the party had left Isaac and were travelling north again, Zebulun said to Jacob, "I wish Grandfather had told us more about what happened when God told Great-grandfather Abraham to kill him. I wanted to know all the details: how close the knife was; what it felt like being tied up on an altar, waiting to be killed."

"Well, I'm glad you didn't ask," replied Jacob, quietly. "My father really is still distressed by memories of that incident, and he does still fear El Shaddai much more than Great-grandfather Abraham did – or than I do, for that matter. God is frighteningly powerful, and a wise man will fear him, but El Shaddai was the friend of my grandfather Abraham, yet he is the fear of my father. It's better not to ask too many questions about it. Dad never liked us asking about it when we were young."

❧

A young man of sixteen strode across the field carrying a toddler on his shoulders. The toddler was smiling and laughing, with the occasional shout of joy as his mount jumped into the air or suddenly stopped and spun around and around.

"Doot again, Doseph," said the toddler once after being tipped upside down, Joseph's firm grip on his legs preventing him from falling off.

"Oh, but you're getting heavier, Ben," responded his brother. "You're much too heavy now for me to hold you upside down like this." He stopped and bent over until Benjamin's short hair swept the grass which was kept closely cropped by the mottled sheep that were lying nearby.

Benjamin's chubby arms reached up to his head, trying unsuccessfully to grab the grass that brushed his hair. After a while, Joseph stood up again and said, "We need to go home now, Ben."

"Home!" responded Benjamin cheerfully, stretching out one hand towards the collection of tents that could be seen some distance away. Joseph walked most of the way with his brother on his shoulders, then he lowered him to the ground and they walked the remaining distance to the camp side by side. Joseph still missed his mother very much, but Benjamin was a close connection to her and he did his best to show him both companionship and leadership.

In a family of twelve boys, it shouldn't have been possible to be lonely, but Joseph was. None of his brothers shared his attitudes or interests. None of them had a feeling for God like his, nor were they willing to worship as he wanted to.

His strongest friendship was with his father, and he felt most useful when he was spending time with Benjamin, telling him stories about Abraham and Isaac and their God. Already Benjamin could answer the simple questions that Joseph asked about God and his promises. The camp was always full of talk about God, but Joseph felt that most of his brothers viewed God as a mere decoration in their life. Joseph considered God the centre of his life, the one with whom he could walk.

☙

They arrived at the tents and Jacob greeted them, "Shalom, Joseph; shalom, little Ben." He swung his youngest son into the air and then sat him on his hip, as Rachel had always done with Joseph. Jacob still missed Rachel every day, and found that life still seemed a little empty without her. But with Joseph he felt there was a sharing of spirit that grew with time, and he looked forward to bringing him into the leadership of the family. Joseph was just the right sort of person to be a good leader.

Once Jacob had Benjamin seated comfortably, he turned to Rachel's older son.

"Well, Joseph," he said, "you are almost seventeen now, and when you are, there will be some changes in the camp."

"Can I start to care for the sheep then, father?" asked Joseph, eagerly.

"Yes, you can, but that is not all you will be doing. I have other plans for you, too. Something new."

"What are they?" Joseph asked, intrigued. Younger children aren't often used for new things in a family. Mostly, they just follow in the footsteps of their older siblings, always reaching up to maturity perhaps, but along a well-trodden path, not an exciting road of originality.

"They are plans, my son. Plans I have had for a few years, but I am not going to explain them quite yet. Not until you are seventeen."

Chapter 14

Seventeen

Jacob was as good as his word. When Joseph turned seventeen, he took his place with his brothers in keeping the family livestock. First he went to help look after the sheep and goats, an occasion which stirred Jacob's memory again. More than thirty years before, he had met Rachel for the first time while she was looking after her father's sheep. He remembered his bravado in single-handedly rolling back the stone that covered the well so that Rachel could water her flock. And now she was gone, and their son was taking on the care of his flocks. Jacob had kept Joseph back from this task a little longer than the other brothers, feeling that Joseph might need a bit of caring for amongst his brothers. Their jealousy of him had been obvious for many years, and Jacob didn't want it to lead to anything serious.

But now, Joseph was seventeen and Jacob wanted him to learn about the flocks as quickly as possible, and then take over complete responsibility for their care. He trusted Joseph and his decisions. Reuben was the oldest, but he lacked both strength of character and stability. Simeon and Levi were too hard. In all honesty, he did appreciate their willingness to enforce what they believed to be right, but their actions were not always properly thought through and sometimes caused trouble. That matter of Shechem the son of Hamor had almost brought disaster on the family – although he had been quite pleased with their resolution in the end. But if God hadn't taken care of them, who knew what might have happened?

Dan and Naphtali and Gad and Asher were the sons of the servant girls, and, while he certainly counted them as his sons and loved them, he didn't want them leading the family. In fact, he had doubts about their character too. He was looking forward to hearing Joseph's response to their work as shepherds. They would be his first companions in the fields, caring for the sheep together.

Jacob had more confidence in Judah than in most of his sons, but he was busy much of the time looking after his own family. Although Judah still helped with looking after the family flocks at times, he was understandably more focused on trying to build up his own flocks. It just wouldn't work for him to try doing both jobs.

Issachar and Zebulun were the only ones left: Leah's two youngest sons, just a little older than Joseph – but how different they were from Joseph! Joseph was a natural-born leader, and a hard worker, too. Issachar and Zebulun might do the job well enough; he didn't know. That was really the point: they just didn't stand out from their brothers, and would have no chance of commanding respect from them.

No, Joseph it would have to be – but how would his brothers respond when Jacob made his intentions clear?

CR

It didn't take long for Joseph to sum up the first group of his brothers. He worked with Dan and Naphtali and Gad and Asher for about two months before concluding that he had learned all he could from them. He then waited another two months in the hope that things would improve before reporting his opinion of their work to his father.

When Joseph made his report, he was as forbearing as he could be while still telling his father the truth. The fact was that his brothers did not do their work well. Sheep were often being left unattended, and they weren't always being guided to good food and water either. Joseph reported that there had been a few cases where sheep had been killed by wild beasts and the brothers had not been there to protect them or even report the deaths. Leading the sheep to the best available food and making sure that they had all the water they needed took quite a bit of consistent work, and Joseph believed that his brothers were too quick to rest when the welfare of the sheep should have been their first concern.

This report was not made until after Joseph had tried to convince his brothers to improve their work. He showed them what was wrong and suggested ways to fix it, but they didn't shape up. As far as they were concerned, the problem was Jacob's, and if he didn't supervise them, they would get away with whatever they could – that was part of the game. Joseph tried in vain to convince them that in cheating their father, they were cheating themselves: the sheep were their own food and income. Healthy, well-fed sheep grew better wool and made better meat; they sold for higher prices, or fed more of the family despite slaughtering fewer animals. Thus Joseph argued – and Joseph was a very articulate young man, well able to mount a convincing argument about anything – but his brothers simply sneered. After that, Joseph had carried the burden of caring for the flock himself and doing the extra work he saw was necessary. After just two months, the results were already showing in the flock, with the sheep putting on weight more quickly and looking healthier.

Jacob was pleased with the whole experiment. Joseph had discovered the rules of being a shepherd without even being shown a good example. He had assessed the situation correctly and drawn the right conclusions. Not only that, but he had not rushed into judgement and condemnation of his brothers – instead, he had tried to guide them to a better solution, and made a negative report only when they refused to change.

Joseph had earned his father's approval, both as a son and as a successful worker. A special coat was made at Jacob's orders and presented to Joseph with his father's blessing.

Needless to say, his brothers were not impressed. A special coat with long sleeves and bright colours announced to all that Joseph was better than the rest of them. That was never going to make them happy, even if one or two of them could see some justice in the reward. After all, it was a fair reflection of his attitude to work and his success in improving the flock so markedly in such a short time.

Jacob put all the family flocks back together again and appointed Joseph to make the plans for pasturing them. He was also to instruct his brothers in their work so as to keep the animals safe and optimise their development. Since Joseph had no experience with goats, he started by seeking advice from his older brothers, but they viewed his questions as patronising condescension and refused to help. In fact, they rarely spoke to Joseph at all, and when they did it was always with the rash speech of anger and hatred.

Dan and Naphtali, Gad and Asher learned nothing from the experience, deliberately ignoring the instructions they were given. Joseph frequently found them lying on their backs, sleeping in the sunshine while the sheep wandered freely without protection.

Chapter 15

Dreaming

Just a few weeks later, Joseph had a dream. He was in the field harvesting grain with his brothers. They were all gathering the cut stalks and tying them in sheaves when a funny thing happened. He put his sheaf on the ground ready to collect another, when suddenly it stood up, all by itself. That was strange enough, but then the sheaves that his brothers had laid down also stood up and gathered in a circle around his sheaf. Once the circle was complete, the eleven encircling sheaves all bowed long and low to his sheaf of grain.

He woke from sleep and lay there, feeling good for a while, revelling in his own importance despite the strange way in which it had been shown. Children with many older siblings are rarely shown much respect by their siblings, and this family was worse than many because jealousies existed between wives as well as between their children.

Joseph lay back in the darkness and thought about the dream, reflecting on the curious fact that little Benjamin had been among the brothers in his dream, although he was much too young to work in the fields with his brothers.

Should he tell his brothers about the dream?

Later that day he told them. He hadn't really intended to, but they had sneered at his special coat and then laughed at his dead mother, and for a few moments he had wanted to get back at them. It probably wasn't the best thing he could have done, but he described the dream to them in detail, emphasising how they had all bowed down to him, every last one of them.

Naturally, it wasn't the only reason why they hated him. They had already hated him for various reasons, some of which he had no control over anyway – and the ones he could control he wouldn't have changed, except perhaps for telling them about the dream. They hated him because he was honest and reliable, hardworking and truthful, capable and good-looking – all of which showed them in a bad light.

They all knew that if work needed doing, Joseph would not only do it reliably, but well – better than they would. In many cases they secretly feared that he would do it better than they could even if they tried as hard as they could – which they rarely did.

So Joseph was always a reproach to them, incessant and obvious. Their father noticed and honoured Joseph above them, and even their doting mothers made pointed remarks about it at times.

Only the brothers agreed that it was all Joseph's fault, so they often discussed it together. They all agreed that they were treated most unfairly and that Joseph was constantly trying to make them look bad. He was, they all agreed, a sneak, a show-off, a cheeky upstart, a braggart and, most importantly, *not one of them.*

As for Joseph, he wasn't sure whether the dream came from his own mind, showing a pride that he didn't like, or was put into his head by God with a message of truth. Only time would tell.

❧

Wheat harvest came and went, but Joseph didn't forget the dream he had had. Nor did his brothers, and their hatred continued to poison their attitude toward him.

There was the incident during the harvest, when they were all binding sheaves, just as in his dream. Judah had come to help with the reaping, and maybe that had made it worse.

Joseph had just finished tying up a sheaf and had stood it up beside a stack of other sheaves, when Simeon came along, picked up the sheaf, threw it down on the ground and walked on it. Levi was with him and pretended to be looking away, so that when he too walked on Joseph's sheaf it seemed completely accidental. Simeon then looked toward Joseph with a sneer and walked away.

Joseph quietly picked up the maltreated sheaf and straightened it up a bit before standing it with the other sheaves once more. But soon afterwards Judah came along with Gad and Asher and, in standing up his own sheaf, knocked over Joseph's so that it lay on the ground again. With an appearance of casual unconcern, he turned around a little, glancing towards Joseph to make sure that he was aware of what was happening. Then he looked up into the sky as if to watch a bird flying overhead. As he continued to look up, he took a step or two backwards, treading on Joseph's sheaf. His feet moved backwards and forwards a little and the plaited stalks used to tie up the sheaf began to give way. Gad was evidently pretending to look up at the same bird as he took a step or two forward and stood on the sheaf to hold it in place while Judah casually scuffed his feet around, gradually spreading the stalks Joseph had so carefully gathered.

Joseph moved hurriedly towards Judah to minimise the damage. "Hey, I'll take that, Judah," he protested, but as he reached down to grab the sheaf, Judah stepped forward and gave him a push. It was not a gentle push, and Joseph lost his balance and fell to the ground.

"Oh no you won't," growled Judah, "you'll take what we give you!" Then he and Gad picked up Joseph's sheaf and dropped it on him as he lay helpless on the ground. "So now our sheaves are all standing up, and you and your sheaf are grovelling at our feet."

"And that seems fair," said Gad.

"...because you are just about the youngest, and, look, you can't even tie up a sheaf properly," finished Asher, reaching down and yanking at the restraining stalks until they finally came undone. The sheaf came apart completely and Joseph was covered in a flood of wheat stalks.

The brothers had all been watching and laughed together loudly as Joseph stood up, brushed off the stalks from his clothes and began to put the sheaf back together again. He was furious, but he knew that anger wouldn't fix the problem.

As Joseph finished tying up the ruined sheaf for the second time, Judah spoke, threateningly: "And, Joseph, don't you dare tell Dad about this or you'll regret it. Understand?"

Joseph never did tell Jacob. Maybe if Jacob had known, things might have been different just a few weeks later.

Anyway, the wheat harvest was over when Joseph had another dream, and this one upset not only his brothers, but also his father. As Joseph recounted the dream to Jacob, he had been standing up in the sky, and from that elevated position he had seen the sun, the moon and eleven stars bowing down to him. He couldn't really describe *how* any of these things had bowed, but bow they had, and he had been the only one left standing.

Jacob had no difficulty interpreting the dream, and the interpretation left him a little annoyed.

"I don't like your dream, Joseph. Shall I and your mother and your brothers really bow down to you? Where do you get such dreams?"

"I don't know where they come from, Dad," Joseph replied, "but they seem very real and I don't feel as if I could ever forget them."

Jacob mulled the matter over in his mind, irritated, but wondering.

Joseph's brothers weren't wondering at all. This was the last straw.

Chapter 16

Betrayed

"Here he comes; it's the dreamer!"

It was Naphtali who saw Joseph first. To own the truth, they had all been waiting for him, keeping a close eye out for him. None of them would ever have admitted it, but that was the real reason why they were in this wild, dry place where none but the occasional caravan would ever pass. It was not really a good place for the flocks, with little grass and even less water; and, of course, the pits were quite dangerous. But it was the pits that appealed to several of the brothers. The delightful picture of Joseph lying helpless at the bottom of a pit, surrounded by the brothers he had said would all bow down to him, had taken such a tight hold of their imaginations that they couldn't even begin to ask whether what they planned was fair.

For most of the brothers it was hardly even a choice: they hated Joseph and here was an opportunity to get rid of him. What could they do but take it?

Reuben was the only one with a slightly more moderate attitude. Oh, for sure, he didn't like Joseph, but *killing* him because of that? – It was more than he could justify. He alone had suggested a plan that didn't include killing Joseph just as soon as they could lay their hands on him.

Judah had moved past that, however. For him, not only was Joseph as good as dead, but he had begun to wonder if there was any way to get some advantage from disposing of his brother.

Well aware of their hatred, but in happy ignorance of the fact that most of them had every intention of turning hatred into homicide, Joseph approached his brothers unconcernedly, quite pleased with their unexpected willingness to travel large distances to make sure the flock was well-fed.

As he approached, they all stood to meet him. The slightly amusing thought passed through Joseph's head that maybe they were making sure they stood so that he couldn't think they were bowing down before him.

Joseph stepped among his brothers with never a moment's suspicion that the events of the next few moments were to change the rest of his life beyond recognition and so degrade his brothers that they would never be able to forget their betrayal of him.

Each of the brothers would have liked someone else to launch the attack, but finally it was Simeon and Levi who made the first move. Each grabbed one of Joseph's arms and Judah warned him not to struggle or he would regret it. The rest of his brothers then stepped forward and surrounded him before lifting him and carrying him to the side of one of the pits. It was dry and not too deep, which would keep Reuben happy, but it was certainly too deep for Joseph to get out without assistance.

"Let's get that special coat off him," said Simeon. "We'll need it." He grabbed the collar of the coat and pulled it roughly off Joseph's shoulders and down to his elbows.

Levi looked at him questioningly, but said nothing, instead helping to pull the sleeves off Joseph's arms one by one.

Simeon took the colourful coat and rolled it up, leaving Joseph standing in his simple tunic, a frightened young man encircled by implacable enemies.

They pushed him into the pit and then spread out around the edge, looking pitilessly down on this upstart of a brother who thought he could rule over them all. Bow down before him? – Here was the truth of it, they thought, as they all looked down on him and he stared up at them in terror. It didn't make them feel even a little bit guilty when he begged them to set him free. There was just the feeling of enjoying a well-earned victory.

Nine of the brothers enjoyed their sneering at Joseph, but Reuben was still trying to work out exactly how he could get all of his brothers to leave Joseph alone so that he could free him and return him safely to their father.

After a while, the brothers decided to go back to their camp and eat, so Joseph was left alone with his thoughts, but without food and without hope.

As the other brothers brought out their food, Reuben announced that he would take the sheep to water, and began to lead them away alone. He led the flock past the pit where Joseph was and quickly ran and looked in.

"Joseph," he called softly, and Joseph looked up in sudden hope. "I'm going to do my best to arrange to free you and take you home. Don't tell anyone."

"Oh, yes. Please help me," breathed Joseph.

Reuben glanced uneasily over his shoulder to make sure that none of his brothers had seen his actions and ran quickly to rejoin the sheep, as they trotted eagerly towards the nearby well.

This young man, Reuben, described by his father as "unstable as water", was the only one of the brothers with any feeling of compassion or care for a suffering brother. But although the others felt no remorse yet, guilt would soon flourish in their minds, and they would live with it gnawing at them constantly for more than twenty years.

CR

Reuben and Joseph were both racking their brains for any way to deliver Joseph from the hopeless situation he was in.

Reuben had taken the flocks to the well, seeking silence in which to think. At the same time, he didn't want to be away for too long in case his earlier arguments against killing Joseph were forgotten by the more bloodthirsty of his brothers.

Joseph was sitting at the bottom of a dry pit, struggling with fear. Surely his brothers wouldn't actually kill him? Occasionally, he could hear their voices as they laughed and joked over their meal. Was there any way to climb out of this hole?

Time after time, he tried to scale the wall, but the isolated footholds and handholds were too small and too far apart to allow him to get anywhere near the top. And even if he did get out, what chance would there be of escape? Ten against one weren't odds that gave him much hope. Even with Reuben's help, it wasn't much better – he had often seen Simeon, Levi and Judah banding together to override their oldest brother's opinion. He didn't give up, because that wasn't Joseph's way, but his repeated efforts led only to constant failure.

He sensed that the sound of his brothers' meal had changed, and redoubled his efforts to escape. His scrabbling fingers were desperately searching for a handhold higher than he had ever managed before, only a couple of metres below the top of the pit, when he heard footsteps above and a voice said, "Well, well, well, look who's trying to escape." It was Simeon's voice, and Joseph's heart dropped.

"This is the lad," came Judah's voice. "Healthy and strong, as you can see. You'll need to make sure that you keep an eye on him."

Simeon picked up a stone and stood over Joseph. "Get down," he said harshly, "or I'll drop this on you."

Joseph tried to climb down, but lost his footing and fell the last metre or so, landing awkwardly on his feet before stumbling and falling on his backside. He stood up again slowly, rubbing his hands.

Five other men were standing with his brothers on the edge of the pit, looking down at him keenly. One of them asked, "So this is your brother, is it?"

"Our half-brother," corrected Judah, carefully. "The son of another woman who is now dead."

"But you want to sell him as a slave?" asked another of the strangers.

Joseph listened in growing disbelief. Who were these men and why were they talking about slaves? Were his brothers really talking about selling him? Surely they couldn't do anything so awful?

"Yes – he's impossible to have around. Does nothing but cause trouble, so it's best to get rid of him."

"You would really sell your brother as a slave?" asked the third stranger. They all seemed to be having difficulty believing their ears.

"Look, if you had him as a brother, you would understand," said Simeon.

"And anyway, he's not our brother, he's our half-brother," insisted Levi.

"He keeps telling us how great he is," said Judah.

"And getting us into trouble with our father," added Gad.

"But, selling your brother?" repeated the first stranger, incredulously.

"Well, you're talking about trading him as a slave," retorted Judah, "and he's your relative too. Not very distant either: about a second cousin, I would guess. Don't try to sound so very self-righteous and kind yourselves!"

"I suppose so," replied another stranger, and Joseph wondered who they were. Relatives, clearly, but there were a few different groups of relatives around. These men didn't look like any of the men he had seen with Uncle Esau so long ago when they had returned from Paddan-aram. Maybe they were descendants of Ishmael or one of Great-grandpa Abraham's other sons. He hoped they would take pity on him, but it seemed more likely that they wouldn't, with all this talk of slaves.

"Let me go," he begged. "I'm your brother, not a slave to be bought and sold."

"Be quiet," said Judah, and Simeon again picked up the stone that he had threatened to drop on Joseph a few moments before.

Joseph decided it would be wise to keep quiet, for a while at least. What had happened to Reuben and his plans?

"Well, what do you want for him?" asked one of the strangers.

"What are you willing to give?" countered Judah.

"He hasn't had any practice being a slave, and that means he'd be likely to give trouble," said the leader. "We'd have to watch him carefully all the way to Egypt, and spend time teaching him submission. It all adds up to hard work, and then we probably won't get much for him because he won't know how to stand on the sale platform. In fact, the more I think about it, the more I reckon he's not worth taking."

"I think you're right," agreed one of his associates. "We'd be better off without him. He wouldn't sell for much, and he'd cause too much trouble on the way. Let's just leave him and go."

"Now that doesn't make sense," said Simeon. "You'd be missing a wonderful opportunity. He really is smart and strong. It's obvious to anyone that he is something special. Just look at his eyes – they're not the eyes of a moron. He's friendly and helpful, too. Not only that, but he's really good at organisation and planning."

Joseph listened to this description of his talents with surprise and deep sorrow. Simeon had never before admitted that he had any good features at all, let alone the skills he listed now. It was ironic how wonderful he was once his brothers could see a way of getting some money for him – and getting rid of him.

The strangers obviously saw the same irony, and they looked at Simeon with sardonic smiles. He had the grace to look a little shamefaced, but tried to justify himself with the explanation: "He really does have some rather special characteristics, it's just that he doesn't fit in with our family. The Egyptians will be glad to have his abilities and he'll recoup for you every last shekel you spend on him."

The discussion continued for a few minutes, and finally a price was agreed on to sell Joseph as a slave. His brothers lowered a rope to him and lifted him out of the pit, watching him carefully as he climbed awkwardly out onto level ground. Joseph decided that it was not possible to escape with so many people around and stood quietly as the deal was finalised. Judah took the money, since the sale had been his idea in the first place. They would share it out amongst themselves later.

A rope was put around Joseph's neck and he was taken to where a group of camels stood patiently waiting. Obviously a caravan had been passing when Judah had conceived his money-making idea. The traders had several other slaves with them, all walking with manacles around their necks, hands and feet, and some more chains were quickly found for Joseph.

No-one could tell what the brothers thought as they watched Joseph being chained and added to the line of slaves who would walk behind the camels all the way to Egypt.

"Which way are you going?" asked Simeon as the leader finally mounted his camel and it lurched clumsily to its feet. "Remember to keep away from Hebron. We don't want his father to see him – ah, although he would probably be glad to see him go anyway."

"Yes, we'll keep away," said the leader. "We're not risking losing our merchandise."

The camels began to walk away, and the manacled slaves followed as the leading chain pulled at their necks. At the end of the line, Joseph too was jerked into motion.

"Shall we look out for you all next time we are passing?" called out the leader sarcastically as the caravan left, his voice floating back to them on the breeze. "Maybe another one of you will be for sale by then!"

Chapter 17

Pain

He had sent a man ahead of them,
Joseph, who was sold as a slave.
His feet were hurt with fetters;
his neck was put in a collar of iron.[11]

Joseph didn't know it then, and neither did his brothers, but Joseph was travelling down to Egypt to save his family. But first, all of the family would have to go through plenty of pain.

The pain started immediately for Joseph. Long before the caravan had left Canaan, he had learned much about the pain of an iron collar. The iron fetters on his legs were heavy too, and chafed badly as he trudged along behind the camels. Chains restrained his hands, and there were many times when he thought of his brothers and wished he could change places with them – Simeon and Judah in particular. It would do them good to walk as slaves to Egypt.

Reuben suffered a little pain too, when he returned to the pit only to find Joseph gone. His plans had failed; he

---

[11] Psalm 105:17-18

had taken too long. He worried that they would all live to regret this deed.

Jacob was the next to feel pain.

The old man, 108 years of age, was told a story by his sons that would curdle the blood of any loving father. It was Simeon, Levi and Judah, the most vocal of the brothers, who told the story. The uncertainty, sympathy and sorrow in their voices were all too convincing as they presented Joseph's special coat, torn and bloody. A shocked father felt pain for his son, for himself and for his family. Joseph had always been his favourite, and not only because Rachel was his mother. Joseph was the best of the best. No father he knew had ever been blessed with a son like Joseph, and now he was dead: torn to pieces. Never would his wonderful character lead his family in wisdom and righteousness. Jacob sobbed as he thought of Joseph's potential and how his brilliance could have led the family in taking over the land that God had promised to Abraham and Isaac. Once again he reviewed the failings of his other sons when measured against the yardstick of Joseph: Reuben could never lead like that; Simeon and Levi would spend all their time slaughtering as they had done with Shechem and Hamor; Judah would try to make it a business; and the sons of Bilhah and Zilpah could never be relied on to do anything. He had nothing against Issachar and Zebulun, but that was just it: they were nothing. No leadership, no guidance, no strength, no courage – forever overshadowed by their older brothers as Joseph had never been.

Only Benjamin was left and he was far too young. And now, he was the only son of Rachel that Jacob had left. He must never be risked in anything dangerous.

Leah and her maid Zilpah felt sorrow at the death of Joseph, but their sorrow was mingled with a touch of relief. Joseph was a delight, to be sure, but he had still been competition for their sons, and both Leah and

Zilpah knew that their sons had hated Joseph. Not only that, but the boys had all endured cavalier treatment at Jacob's hands because of the presence of Joseph. Surely they would be treated more favourably now that he was dead?

Bilhah's sons had also been on the receiving end of criticism because of Joseph. But she had loved Rachel, her beautiful mistress, and Joseph, Rachel's son, had truly been a wonderful teenager, so mature and helpful.

Three-year-old Benjamin was the next one to feel pain. Joseph was his idol – he positively worshipped his big brother. Benjamin was sure that no-one had ever had a better brother than Joseph. He could always be relied upon to be patient and to play all sorts of games with his little brother. Benjamin felt like a king with Joseph's willing gifts of time and companionship.

Jacob told him as gently as he could. "Joseph has had an accident, Benjamin," he said, as he sat Benjamin on his lap and hugged him.

"I kiss him better. Fix him!" said Benjamin, trying to slide off Jacob's knee so that they could go to his beloved brother.

"No, we can't go to him," Jacob mourned, and his eyes were full of tears again.

"What's wrong, Daddy?" asked Benjamin in concern. He looked up at his father and reached up with his fingers to brush away the tears that welled from his eyes.

Then Jacob could control himself no longer. He broke down and wept, while Benjamin looked up at him with sympathy.

"What's wrong, Daddy?" he repeated. "Has you hurt you-self?"

Jacob folded the child in his arms and hugged him tightly as he sobbed until he found a little control for his grief. Then he explained to Benjamin what had happened to his brother: not the whole truth, but enough to bring the tragedy into the heart of this child too.

Pain was in their hearts, and the pain would not go away. Jacob was sure that the pain would bring him to an untimely death, but maybe that was just what he hoped. Life held too much pain, and everything that had ever brought him joy seemed to have gone.

Rachel was gone. Joseph was gone. Only Benjamin was left, and he could not bring Jacob any joy either, for his own pain was too great for his childish heart to comprehend. Whenever Benjamin looked around for Joseph, that reliable and ever-so-grown-up playmate, he was not there, and the tears flowed again.

All this pain had come from the hatred and jealousy that had taken root, flourished and flowered in the hearts of ten brothers solely because they knew that Joseph was better than they were themselves.

And the hatred and jealousy still lodged in their hearts. When they saw the pain their unnatural behaviour had caused, their response was not sympathy, sorrow or guilt – not yet. Rather, it was an even greater hatred and jealousy, and a feeling of being ill-used: nobody, they were sure, would have mourned like that for them. They were probably right, and at that time, they had never given anyone any reason to do so. In time, God would begin to work within them, but that could only happen once they started to question themselves.

Chapter 18

A slave must obey

The Way of the Sea led the caravan towards Egypt. Joseph learned much as they went, but some of the change was simply overwhelming.

A favourite son knows his place in the world, and it is a place of privilege. Joseph was not excessively proud or greedy, but he knew that his opinions were simply more important than those of others. The experience of years had shown him that.

Not only that, but he knew that if his brothers ever treated him badly, all he had to do was complain and they would receive the retribution they deserved.

Now, suddenly, all that had changed. A slave must obey. His opinions are not important, his suffering evokes no sympathy, and any mistreatment is simply what anybody would expect. Since a slave belongs to his master, a master will not deliberately lower the value of his investment, but most incidental damage done to a slave will repair itself with time.

Joseph was now a slave, and must learn to listen carefully to instructions and to obey as quickly as possible. One morning early on, he refused to move when the caravan started off. The man in front of him stood up and walked, which tightened the chain around Joseph's neck.

Soon he had been pulled off his feet and was being dragged along the ground by the chain around his neck. But his weight made it difficult for the man in front of him to walk, and the leader quickly stopped the caravan. The slavers knew just what to do – new slaves often caused trouble like this. A few strokes of the whip made sure that they had Joseph's attention, and then his chain was connected directly to the saddle of another camel. When the caravan moved off again and Joseph still refused to walk, the chain tightened around his neck, pulled him over, and dragged him along. It quickly became clear that if he didn't start walking, either his neck would be broken or the rough ground would quickly reduce him to a bloody pulp. He had to struggle desperately for a few moments to stand up, but from then on, he walked when he was told to. Slowly the lacerated skin recovered and the welts from the whip healed. The pain in his mind took longer to subside.

By the time they arrived in Egypt he had learned the most important lessons of being a slave.

He learned that if a slave is consistently quicker and more obedient than other slaves, he will be treated better. Joseph was quick to obey.

He learned that a slave that talks back to his master often feels the lash. Joseph obeyed without arguing.

He also noticed that slaves always waited to be told what to do, and he decided to try an experiment. He thought ahead and tried to predict what his master would order next. Much of the time this was very easy, and Joseph made sure he pre-empted his master's commands whenever possible, so that whatever the man wanted was done before he asked. Joseph found that if he did this, he was treated more kindly than the other slaves. But it required humility. Acknowledging that he was no longer important was the hardest thing he had to learn, but during the long, lonely nights as he slept under the stars, he decided to choose humility as a way of life – at least for the time being. He still liked to count the stars, but he couldn't help wondering whether he fitted into God's promises to Abraham any more than did the slave traders who were leading him to Egypt to sell.

Joseph was able to make very sensible choices which made his life much better than it would have been otherwise, but he still struggled to understand why any of this was happening to him. Had his dreams just been ordinary dreams? They had seemed too special for that, somehow, but could he be sure they were predictions from God? Would he ever see his brothers again? It didn't seem likely, but God had a way of achieving the impossible. After all, Sarah had borne Isaac, her only son, when she was 91 years old, which was simply beyond the realms of possibility – unless there was a God who could work in the realm of impossibility. What would happen to him? He didn't know what to expect as a slave. Could he escape? Maybe it would be better to wait until he was in the house of an owner. There were sure to be opportunities to escape if he waited a while. But what if he got a cruel master who beat him often? He might not live long enough to escape.

The caravan made its way up the Nile River until they reached their goal – the slave market where their stock would be sold and all the costs recouped. Other trading goods would be sold for healthy profits too, lining the purses of the Ishmaelite and Midianite traders with silver.

Egypt was always looking for slaves – there was work that no Egyptian was willing to do. As the caravan approached this centre of civilisation, the slaves were prepared for sale: a little more food, and a little less physical punishment too – if it could be avoided.

By that time, although he had only been with the caravan for a little over three weeks, Joseph was almost never struck, and his chain was rarely pulled to hurry him up. Instead, he was relied on to set a good example for the other slaves and to encourage them to cooperate where possible.

Although Joseph did not know it, the leader seriously considered keeping him as his personal slave instead of selling him in Egypt. Had there been no family connection between them, he would probably have done so, but he couldn't quite accept the idea of keeping a relative as a slave. No, it was better to sell him quickly and forget all about it.

So Joseph stood on the stage with the rest where he could be seen by the buyers – his height and strong physique marking him out as a desirable lot. The traders were pleased to see several rich and powerful citizens waiting for the lots to be presented. Everyone knew that the best lots were kept until last, and by the time Joseph was pushed to the front of the platform, all of the other slaves with whom he had walked from Canaan had been sold to various different owners.

"Here is a young Hebrew: obedient, tall, strong and clever. We have sold many slaves, but we have never seen one like this before. He works with a smile, and it's almost as if he reads your mind. He has already done what you want before you tell him to! When you bid for this young man, you are buying many years of faultless service."

Joseph listened to the words as they were spoken, but not a one did he understand. The spiel was all in the Egyptian tongue, and suddenly he felt a rising panic. He was being sold as a slave and he couldn't even understand how they were presenting him. He would be bought by an owner who would give him instructions he could not understand. What hope would he have of pleasing an owner who didn't even speak the right language?

Although Joseph didn't understand it, the responses to him as a slave were all very positive and the bidding was brisk. When the sale was finally made, a large amount of money changed hands. Potiphar, the captain of Pharaoh's guard – Joseph's new master – was hopeful that this would prove to be the best slave he had ever purchased.

Over time, Potiphar's hopes were satisfied, but it was not without trouble, and the trouble started straight away.

"Come, boy," said Potiphar to Joseph, gesturing with his hand. "How old are you?"

Joseph understood the gesture and walked across to his new master. But the question was garbled nonsense as far as he was concerned, and he could do nothing but shrug. The leader of the trading caravan handed the rope to Potiphar and did something he had never done before after selling a slave. He said goodbye.

℞

No sooner had the slave trader walked away than Potiphar encountered his first problem. He asked Joseph where he was from, and received only a confused look in reply. He tried again, but eventually realised that he had bought a slave who could not even understand his language. He wondered whether he should send a servant to demand his money back from the trader, but he was afraid that he would look foolish, since really, it should have been obvious. Foreigners spoke so many different languages and never seemed to understand his language – despite its simplicity of vocabulary and its logical grammar.

He would have to delay his plans for the new slave until he had learned the language – but he had heard that some people never did learn the language. He hoped this one wouldn't be like that.

"What is your name?" he asked, but even that simple question wasn't easy to communicate. It took a few tries of gesturing and trying different words before he could finally understand that his slave's name was Joseph. Then he forgot it straight away anyway. He had always found it rather hard to remember these foreign names, and now he had a new slave whose name he couldn't even remember! His wife would probably laugh at him when she found out.

Potiphar led his new slave along the cobbled road towards Pharaoh's palace, and the buildings they passed became steadily grander and grander. Potiphar said nothing as they went, and Joseph was free to look around in amazement at the enormous buildings. He had never seen buildings one quarter of the size before. In fact, apart from their short time in Succoth, he had lived all of his life in tents, often far from any buildings. These buildings were beyond his comprehension, with pillars that were large enough to hide his whole family behind: parents, children and servants together. He stared open-mouthed at the colourful murals and other decorations that glorified the many gods of Egypt. Potiphar noticed his amazement and smiled, quite content that the architecture of Egypt should inspire such wonder in his slave.

Just before they reached the palace, Potiphar turned off the main concourse and entered his own house. It was a large house, as befitted the captain of Pharaoh's guard. But part of the reason for its size was that it was not only a house: it was also a prison where Pharaoh's prisoners were kept. Political prisoners and prisoners who had personally offended or angered Pharaoh were all confined in this place. Both exquisitely comfortable rooms and dank, airless dungeons could be found in this pile, and Joseph was to spend the next thirteen years of his life in numerous rooms of varying repute on most of the many levels within its walls.

Chapter 19

Potiphar's house

Joseph quickly found that learning his master's language would not be easy. God's separation of people into different languages at Babel had been the single most effective way of dividing people and keeping them separate. And now Joseph was finding out just how hard life could be when communication is well-nigh impossible.

None of Potiphar's slaves spoke Hebrew, but some spoke languages that were quite similar, and it was one of these that Potiphar appointed to help Joseph learn the language.

Joseph had to learn everything word by word, expression by expression, cultural clue by cultural clue, and it challenged his abilities to the utmost. Since everyone knew that the Egyptian language was simple – could not even children learn it easily? – a lack of comprehension was often mistaken for stubbornness. Physical punishment reinforced the importance of learning quickly.

Slowly, or so it seemed to him, Joseph mastered the language. His eyes also told him much of what went on in Potiphar's house. Clearly Potiphar was very popular with his king, his soldiers, his servants and even his slaves – but not with his wife, Zulaykha, who often openly derided him. He saw that Potiphar found her disdain hard to endure, and felt sorry for the man, although he could never have told him so.

Over time, Joseph came to be accepted in the house and his wisdom began to shine through.

Joseph had a deep appreciation of spiritual matters, and his father and mother had given him a firm grounding in the knowledge of El Shaddai, the God of Abraham, Isaac and Jacob. As a child, he had eagerly welcomed any tales of El Shaddai or his angels and the promises made to Abraham and Isaac. When Jacob had told of his own encounters with angels, there had never been a better listener than Joseph.

So from the very earliest age, a gap had existed between Joseph and his brothers. Over time the gap had gradually grown until hatred was almost inevitable. Joseph seemed to make wise decisions naturally, whereas his brothers lacked the foundation to do so. Thus, the gulf between them had widened steadily.

During that traumatic time when Joseph was travelling to Egypt, Reuben had thought of him often. He wondered how Joseph was faring, and sometimes even tried to put himself in Joseph's position, but when he did so, his feelings were wildly wrong.

Reuben imagined anger and rebellion, whereas Joseph, after that first foolhardy refusal to cooperate, had practised patience and cooperation. Reuben dreamed up stories of dangerous adventures with thrilling escapes from the slave traders; of midnight battles that left Joseph's captors coughing out their life in wilderness wastelands. In reality, Joseph had accepted his conditions and tried to make the best of them, trusting that God would be with him.

Even as a slave, Joseph's attitude caught people's attention as he showed the same faith as his father, grandfather and great-grandfather had possessed. Joseph did his best to build on his natural strengths, while his brothers pandered to their weaknesses. They would continue to follow a downward spiral until they chose to change. But that change was not to happen for many years, during which time Joseph would continue to grow and mature. Choices make changes.

Potiphar had started by giving Joseph simple tasks, and quickly found that he worked hard. More important tasks followed, and Potiphar's overseers learned that not only could Joseph be trusted, but that he was blessed with a mind which could easily grasp complex situations while presenting them to others in a simple fashion. Potiphar's slaves learned that if you worked with Joseph, he always worked hard and didn't try to slack off when no-one was watching. He did not try to present his fellow-slaves in a bad light, either, but would support them in any way he could. In short, he was just about the perfect slave.

To anyone looking from outside, it was inevitable that Joseph was going to be given increasingly important tasks and trusted to work with less and less supervision. And so it happened.

After just two years in Egypt, at the ripe old age of nineteen – going on twenty – Joseph was appointed by Potiphar as second in command over his house. Mahu, who was in charge, was an old and trusted retainer – Egyptian of course – but Joseph was his deputy. When considering this unprecedented move of making a slave the second in command, Potiphar thought back on the words of the slave trader describing this slave's exceptional talents. He had taken them with several grains of salt at the time, but just two years had shown that, if anything, the slave trader had underestimated this young man. It was premature, Potiphar knew, but he couldn't help thinking that if the good work continued, Joseph might even become his adopted son in a few years.

Making Joseph second in command in the house drew complaints from many of Potiphar's Egyptian servants and workers, who took the appointment of a slave to supervise them as an affront. But Potiphar managed to convince them to reserve judgement for three months and see how conditions unfolded. He was confident that Joseph's reliability, humility and ability would win over the doubters.

And they did. Joseph's work was exemplary, and the noisiest doubters gradually became some of his most vocal supporters. Mahu still worked hard, but he couldn't help noticing after a while that most of his work was done better if he just handed it over to Joseph. Not only did he do his work well, but Joseph had an amazing knack of making his supervisor look good. He always praised his supervisor's good work and never tried to take the praise for himself, even when the ideas had been his.

He really was, Potiphar told himself over and over again, a most amazing young man.

Once again, Potiphar thanked the gods for sending him such a peerless slave and began to make serious plans for the future.

After another year, the whole household was running so smoothly that Potiphar felt more relaxed and confident than he had ever done before. His wife still criticised him and sneered at him in the most private of matters, but he was able to bear that with tolerable grace due to the prosperity that Joseph's leadership had brought to his house. Even more importantly, Pharaoh was pleased with how the prison was operating, and Potiphar had no doubt that it was Joseph's leadership in the rest of the house that was making the prison so much easier to run.

Potiphar would have made the change eventually, but his hand was forced when Mahu, titular head of administration in the house, died suddenly. Potiphar immediately appointed Joseph to the position, making him head over all that took place in the house.

As he made the appointment, he dwelt on the irony that would see his overall household expenses reduced by appointing Joseph to the position that he had already been filling behind the scenes anyway. The cost reduction was not due to improved efficiency, although he was confident that would follow too, but to the amusing fact that the manager of the entire house would not be being paid for his work. Joseph was a slave: fed and dressed from Potiphar's bounty, but receiving no income at all. Potiphar had always made sure that his house manager and other workmen were paid well so that he would never have any difficulty finding good workers – but now he had the best worker possible appointed to the top job, and working for free. He was absolutely sure that there was no other leader or nobleman in Egypt who had this benefit. He chuckled to himself as he signed the letter that appointed Joseph to the exalted position, and decided that he would have to make sure Joseph was rewarded adequately in other ways. Maybe it was time to consider formally adopting him as his son. He could never have had a better real son anyway.

Chapter 20

Potiphar's wife

Joseph's new position brought him abruptly to the notice of Potiphar's wife. Previously, he had been the force behind the work, the invisible hand behind the visible leadership, but now he was the face of all that was done in the house. And he was a handsome face.

Potiphar's wife, Zulaykha, was young, just a few years older than Joseph himself, and she was not satisfied with her husband. He was in an exalted position in the kingdom, which was why she had been willing to marry him, but in other areas, he left a lot to be desired by her.

Mahu, Joseph's predecessor, had previously done all the work that required any interaction with Zulaykha, but Joseph, calm and efficient, was a much younger and more attractive replacement.

At first, Joseph thought her response to him was just because he was close to her in age. They met quite often, and she was always warm and welcoming, asking him about his background, his family and his experiences as a slave. However, although her initial interest had seemed so kind, it soon became clear that she was looking for something more.

Life is rarely simple, and often when it appears to be, something turns up that makes it anything but simple. That was Joseph's situation. His master had appointed him to the most senior position in the house under Potiphar himself, and he had done so because Joseph was reliable and showed complete integrity. Yet now his master's wife was doing her best to get his attention, spending as much time in his company as she could, when Joseph knew he should be working for Potiphar. Having watched Reuben and Bilhah together, Joseph was fairly sure that it wouldn't stop there unless he made sure it stopped. So he started avoiding Zulaykha – sending others to do any work where he would be likely to meet her.

Joseph continued to work hard in his new position. He had already begun to implement various small changes that would make the work of the slaves and servants a little easier. He had discussed many of these changes with Mahu and gained his agreement that they *should* work, but Mahu had been old and a little tired, content to stick to the tried and trusted ways – particularly if the possible improvements were minimal or would only benefit slaves.

After a week, Zulaykha sent for him.

As Joseph walked along the corridor, he wondered what he should do. It was clear that he couldn't talk to Potiphar about this, but if he didn't, it might look as if he was trying to hide something. He was still mulling over the situation when he reached the room where he had been told to meet Zulaykha. She was not there, but a young servant girl was cleaning the floor.

"Where is our mistress?" asked Joseph. "She summoned me to meet her here."

"The mistress found that she had left something in her room, so she went upstairs to get it," replied the girl. "She said that if you came, I was to tell you to go up and meet her there."

Joseph walked out of the room slowly and paused outside the door. He foresaw problems if he went upstairs to her room, but he couldn't see any easy way to avoid it. Maybe he was wrong – maybe her behaviour really was innocent and he had misunderstood. Very slowly, he climbed the stairs, hoping that he would meet her coming down, but no, there was still no sign of her, and the door to her room was standing open.

Stopping at the top of the stairs, he slowly bent to adjust his sandals, then, just as slowly, straightened up and looked around. There was no-one about and nothing he could do in this area to occupy himself until Zulaykha came out. He wanted to get back to his work, but felt that he couldn't just ignore an order from his master's wife. Yet he didn't want to go into her room, whether he was right in his suspicions or not.

He spent some more time reading a list of deliveries that were to be made that day, and then tried to work out the details of a few more minor changes to the way in which the household operated, but it was hard to concentrate, and he was becoming rather desperate. What should he do?

At that moment, Zulaykha stepped out of her room and immediately saw him. "Ah, Joseph, you are here," she said softly. "I have been waiting for you. Come into my room." Not giving him a chance to answer, she turned and went into her room.

Was he imagining it, Joseph asked himself, or was her voice a little more inviting than normal, perhaps even alluring? Her dress was certainly provocative, but that was normal: Zulaykha always dressed in a revealing way that Joseph would never have wanted any wife of his to dress.

What should he do? He wanted to turn around and run down the stairs, but how could he explain that if she complained to Potiphar? There didn't seem to be any way out.

Slowly, he walked along to the doorway, and there she was, waiting for him, a coy smile playing around the corners of her lips. She stepped back, holding open the door and indicating with a gesture of her slim hand that he should enter.

Doubtfully, he did so: on edge; on guard.

As he passed the door, she closed it and leaned back against it.

It was as if a hunter had closed the jaws of a trap. There was no way of escape. Joseph looked around the room uneasily, trying to decide what to do. It was not a very large room, but walking to the centre took him well beyond her reach, so he stopped there and waited.

Zulaykha looked at him and smiled a confident smile as she took a few steps towards him and reached out her hands, saying, "Come to bed with me, Joseph."

"No," said Joseph, but even to his own ears, his voice sounded strangled.

"Oh, but why not? Potiphar is much too old for me, and we both know what else is wrong with him."

Joseph managed to find his voice: "Well, because of me, my master has no concern about anything in the house, and he has put everything that he has in my charge. He doesn't worry about anything except the food that he eats — everything else he leaves up to me. He is not greater in this house than I am, nor has he kept back anything from me except you, because you are his wife. How then can I do this great wickedness and sin against God?"

"What do you mean, 'wicked'? Isn't it wicked to chain me to someone like him?"

"Zulaykha," said Joseph, "you are his wife and he trusts me. It would be wicked for me to do this. I must go."

Zulaykha was still standing between him and the door.

"But, Joseph, I really need you," said Zulaykha wistfully, reaching out her hands towards him again. "Please think about it and we can talk about it again tomorrow."

"I must go," he repeated urgently, then, avoiding her eager hands, he hurried to the door and left.

Joseph found it very hard to concentrate on his work for the rest of that day. He did his best to keep his mind on important business, but the voice of Zulaykha kept intruding. He went to supervise some redecorating work that was being done at the entrance to the house, but as he looked at the door, he saw Zulaykha again in his mind, leaning against her door and…. He quickly shook his head and went to speak to the work supervisor, but even as he spoke with him, her voice whispered again in his mind.

It was a long afternoon, and when he met Potiphar returning from the barracks of the king's guards, he felt guilty. Guilty for what he knew about Zulaykha's willingness to be unfaithful, guilty because he, Joseph, was the one she had set her eyes on, guilty because it was all wrong and he couldn't do anything to fix it.

That night in the dark, when he should have been sleeping, he continued to think. Joseph had a strong mind and a very active sense of right and wrong, but sometimes even the strongest mind can be tempted by evil. He had won the first battle, but could he win the war? He prayed and struggled for what seemed like hours, and may well have been hours. He had seen firsthand some of the damage that unfaithfulness and impatience could cause. Reuben's infidelity with Bilhah, his father's servant-wife, had caused him to be rejected as the oldest son, to be replaced by Joseph himself. Could Joseph show the same sort of unfaithfulness with his master's wife? Punishment would come, he knew − some secrets can never be kept. And even if the secret could somehow be kept from men, it could not be kept from God. God had been faithful for hundreds of years, and could Joseph excuse unfaithfulness for such short-term gains?

He pictured the body of Shechem, the son of Hamor, as he had seen it once Simeon and Levi had finished with it. Shechem had taken advantage of Dinah, their sister, and taken her into his home, too impatient and overcome by lust to wait for marriage. He had died for his unfaithfulness, and his mutilated body had been left as food for the birds and beasts.

Unfaithfulness stirred strong emotions and retribution was often swift and brutal; but even if it wasn't, even if Shechem had got away with his presumptuous passion, God would still judge it. And God would judge Joseph if he sinned in a similar way.

By the end of the night, Joseph was glad he had resisted Zulaykha's requests and determined to continue to do so. He could not live with himself before Potiphar or before God if he let himself be led into sin in that way.

※

The next day, Joseph made sure that he stayed busy supervising the redecoration work, well away from any servants who might pass on a message from Zulaykha.

It was well into the afternoon, and Joseph was starting to hope that he had avoided the problem for the day, when a servant came out with the message that Zulaykha needed to speak to him.

"Please tell her that I am busy outside," Joseph replied to the servant.

A short time later, the servant was back with another message: "Mistress Zulaykha asks you to come upstairs immediately. Master Potiphar's evening meal has not been arranged, and his wife needs to talk to you about what food is available."

Joseph thanked the servant and drew a deep breath. He didn't want to be hurried into doing anything and stayed for a while talking to the supervisor and thinking deeply. Eventually, he went inside and climbed the stairs. As he walked along the corridor to her room, he reviewed his decisions of the night before and confirmed them in his mind. Then he prayed.

When he reached her door, it was open. Across the room, Zulaykha was reclining gracefully on a graceful couch, watching the door. She had obviously been waiting for him.

"Joseph," she said in a seductive voice. "Come in."

"No, madam, I'm sorry, but I can't," Joseph replied. "I am busy and must get back to my work. Did you need to talk to me about the master's meal?"

"Come in and sit with me, and I will explain," Zulaykha said, patting the couch next to her.

Joseph hurried to answer, "No, I can't. I really must go back out and supervise the redecoration work. Can you explain it for me quickly?"

"Oh, Joseph," she replied, pouting a little, "we did enjoy talking to each other, and I'm sure we will again. Come and sit down."

Joseph looked away down the corridor as if he might have heard someone calling him, then turned back to her. "Sorry again, madam, but I really must go unless you can tell me your message."

"Oh, Joseph dear, you do make things difficult. I spoke to my husband this morning and he said that you could choose the food he ate tonight." She looked at him slyly and he wondered why.

"Is that all, madam?" he asked, puzzled.

"Yes, that is all. Remember that you told me he kept only two things from you: the choice of his food, and me as his wife. He was in a hurry this morning and I asked him if you could choose his food this afternoon." She stopped and looked up at Joseph from under her eyelashes, before saying very softly, "He said 'Yes', Joseph. So you can choose his food, and that leaves just one thing left that you haven't had. Why not take it this afternoon too?" She opened her arms towards him, but Joseph was gone.

CR

Day after day Zulaykha harried Joseph, while carefully making sure that none of the other servants or slaves would notice, using both orders and requests to demand his presence at her door. She asked him to talk to her, to sit with her, to lie beside her, to eat with her; but every day she also repeated her original request.

The day came when, just by chance, all of the men of the house, from Potiphar down, were out of the building – except for Joseph. Perhaps Zulaykha had helped to arrange it, perhaps not; either way, she took advantage of it.

Joseph was working in his office, reviewing the household's food supply and deciding how much should be ordered in time for the next new moon. The records of the amount of flour used in the last month seemed a little improbable, so he went into the main part of the house to investigate the flour bins.

As he walked along the corridor towards the storage rooms, he met Zulaykha, who seemed to be looking for someone. Joseph guessed that it was probably him, but was determined to avoid any contact with her if it was at all possible. She was dressed in one of her more revealing costumes, and Joseph examined his list of stores closely.

"Ah, Joseph," she said, in a business-like tone. "Potiphar has requested you to see him upstairs."

"But the master is away today on the king's business and not expected to return until tomorrow."

"Yes," she agreed, "that was the plan, but he had to return unexpectedly and now he needs to talk to you about some extra requirements from Pharaoh. He was too busy to call you himself and asked me to do so."

Joseph immediately hurried to the stairs and went up to Potiphar's rooms. The outer room was empty, and Joseph strode quickly across the exquisitely tiled floor to the inner room, but a quick glance showed that Potiphar was not there either. Behind him, he heard the door close, and turned quickly around to see Zulaykha standing in front of it with a look of triumph on her face. As she had once before, she leaned back against the closed door, shutting off all possible means of escape for Joseph.

"Joseph, why do you keep avoiding me? Don't you like me?"

"How I feel about you doesn't matter. What you have been suggesting is evil; I cannot do it."

"So you do like me?" she asked, ignoring the second sentence. "I thought I had seen you looking at me."

"I must go."

"Not this time, Joseph," she said confidently. "This time your master is away and there is no-one to disturb us."

She stepped towards him sensuously, and Joseph realised that if he did not escape straight away, he never would.

In a moment, Zulaykha was standing right in front of him, grasping his cloak and looking longingly up into his face. "Come to bed with me, Joseph," she said urgently.

It was a scene that Joseph was to remember for the rest of his life. How he did it, he was never quite sure, but somehow he managed to escape her grasp, running from the room in only his loincloth and leaving her holding his cloak.

"Joseph," she cried in anguish, "don't go!"

But Joseph was gone – running down the stairs, not caring who saw, running out of the door, running, running, running until he reached his own room. Quickly, he closed the door behind him and put on another outer garment. He had escaped, but what would happen next? How long could he continue to evade her? How long would it be before she broke down his willpower and dragged him down the path to death? Desperately he prayed to the God of his father asking for help. It was a prayer that God was to answer in a most unexpected and unpleasant way.

Chapter 21

Potiphar's anger

With difficulty overcoming her shock at his rejection, Zulaykha ran after Joseph. Still carrying his cloak, she followed him down the stairs, her hurrying feet gradually slowing to a walk and finally stopping at the main door of the house. A woman scorned, she stood and looked out after him, and as she stood there, her illicit desire for him hardened into an overwhelming need to punish him.

Hesitating on the threshold, with Joseph's cloak in her hands, she began to bend her inventive mind to finding a way to get back at him, to make him suffer.

Yes, he must be made to pay for his insolence. She turned around and made her way back upstairs, mulling over his offences. By the time she slipped into her room she had worked herself into a cold fury. She planned to arrange his death – if she could.

Joseph's cloak was obviously the best weapon she had. No man would leave his cloak with a married woman unless he had some romantic interest in her. No-one would believe his denials. She began to see a way to report events that would take advantage of that cloak, and felt much better.

The first step was to announce to the world that Joseph had come to her demanding sex, having carefully chosen a time when her husband was away and the men of the house were absent. It was a credible story. She had heard reports of such things happening in the past, which was one of the reasons why rich men always had large numbers of servants and slaves. It was also one of the reasons why slaves were never – ever – put in command in a house: they just couldn't be trusted to leave their master's wife alone. Potiphar had been so sure Joseph was different that he had ignored this basic rule of society. Zulaykha smiled grimly to herself: she could get back at both of them at the same time. Her husband would be shown up as not being able to look after his wife, and Joseph would be shown to be a predatory male who could not be trusted.

It was a beautiful plan.

She took the first step when the older men of the house returned. As would any faithful wife who had been threatened by a marauding man, she told of her fight to protect her virtue and her husband's honour. Her eyes were large and her voice breathless as she creatively recounted the frightening scene she had so recently endured. She appealed for their protection and even managed to get in a dig at her husband, blaming him for Joseph being in the house at all.

Once her exchange with the men was over, she withdrew to her room and reflected contentedly on her performance. Stage one had gone well. The next step was to tell her husband. She fingered Joseph's cloak and imagined his response to her charges. How dare he talk to her about sin? What was he but a slave, anyway? And how dare he reject her? That was the part that hurt most.

Within minutes, the story was all over the house, and probably much further afield as well. But Zulaykha had not counted on the fact that these men knew Joseph – and they knew her. Joseph was not the first young man to have taken her fancy, although he was the first to have refused her advances. While Zulaykha had expected everyone to consider this an open and shut case, the men were not quite sure what to believe. They were sure that this reported behaviour would not be normal for Joseph, but lust has led many men to behave in reckless and foolish ways. But would she have refused Joseph if he had approached her in the way she described? – they were not so sure.

All of them had seen her flirtatious behaviour and provocative dress on previous occasions when a man had caught her eye. Some had noticed her regular summoning of Joseph in recent weeks – and Joseph's frequent worried looks.

In their homes, the men discussed the question with their wives, and their doubts were reinforced. Their wives knew Zulaykha, and they had experienced Joseph as a carefully respectful and utterly chaste young man. Not one could think of even a single case in which his behaviour had been anything other than exemplary. Zulaykha, however, was generally thought to be a coquettish young wife married to an older man who could not satisfy her many desires.

So Potiphar's house was divided. Some, mostly those who were a little jealous of Joseph, claimed to believe Zulaykha, but many found her story hard to believe. Nevertheless, no-one talked to Joseph himself about it, or asked for his side of the story. In some ways, he was a little separate from them: their manager, yet so very young – and a foreigner as well. He was also a self-contained young man, always disturbingly quick to talk about his God, and whether things were right or wrong. No, Potiphar would have to decide for himself. But it was telling that nobody – not even Zulaykha – made a move to have Joseph detained.

Potiphar returned as expected late the following afternoon. He found his wife waiting for him near her room, an excited look in her eyes, and wondered what had happened in his absence.

"That Hebrew slave you brought into the house to mock us and make us look foolish…" began Zulaykha.

"You mean Joseph?" interrupted Potiphar, looking puzzled.

"Yes, that Joseph," replied Zulaykha, spitting out the name as if it left a bad taste in her mouth. "He came into the house yesterday while you were away, and all the men were out of the house, and he tried to fool around with me. Well, naturally, I cried out and, look…" she held up the cloak she had grasped so urgently, "… he left his garment behind and ran out of the house." Zulaykha looked at Potiphar, her eyes demanding an aggrieved response.

Potiphar's mouth fell open in amazement, and Zulaykha couldn't help looking rather self-satisfied. What she didn't realise was that, although he was amazed by the story, his mind immediately began to ask questions that she would not have wanted to answer – not truthfully, anyway.

Potiphar was angry. Zulaykha could see it clearly, and assumed that he must be angry with Joseph for threatening her, but that was not the real truth. In fact, Potiphar was angry about many things. He was angry with himself for ever allowing Joseph to be left alone in the house. He knew his wife. He knew that she was much younger than he and that she wanted to live life at a pace he had left behind in his advancing years. He knew that she could be provocative and even seductive with other men, and had wondered before if it ever went further than that. Potiphar was loth to accuse her of anything, but he was angry with himself for allowing a situation to arise in which his wife could develop any attraction towards Joseph. He was angry with Zulaykha, too, for disturbing his peace after Joseph had given him such comfort in his household. He was angry with the men of the house because of the looks they had given him when he had returned that afternoon – looks of pity and sympathy that he had not understood. Now he did. And he was angry with Joseph for being so young and good-looking.

His discussion with his wife did not last much longer. Potiphar asked Zulaykha to repeat the details, which she did willingly, adding a few extra flourishes that seemed even less like the Joseph he knew. He then left her and went to his rooms to consider his next move.

ℂℛ

Potiphar sat moodily at his desk and pondered the events of the day.

What should he do? Appearances were important and his reputation would be damaged if he was seen to believe a slave above his wife. And if he did that, he would have to take action against her as well. It was not really a possibility. She was not completely bad, he thought, and she was decorative and attractive – exactly the sort of wife a man like him should have. He would just need to make sure that he kept more of an eye on her from now on.

Potiphar sighed. If only he had been left in peace! The attempted rape of a rich married woman by a slave would normally be a capital offence, but this was not a normal case. He was not willing to kill Joseph for an offence that he was by no means convinced Joseph had committed. All of his plans for adoption and inheritance had been destroyed by Zulaykha's folly!

Once again, Potiphar sighed and drummed his fingers on the table. Joseph would say that he should do what was right, but what was 'right' here anyway? How could he be sure?

He supposed that he must go and talk to Joseph about what had happened and see what his explanation was. Tiredly, he stood and went to Joseph's office, where he found him seated at his desk working. As Potiphar entered, Joseph looked up, and the expression of sorrow or pity in his eyes roused Potiphar's anger once more. He did not want sympathy.

"Joseph," he began, trying to keep the anger from his voice, "what happened yesterday? My wife says that you attacked her, but ran away when she screamed. I want you to tell me the truth. You know that I have trusted you and put you in a position in my house that no-one ever appoints a slave to. So, tell me what happened yesterday."

"My lord, you have been very kind to me," replied Joseph slowly, and stopped.

"That didn't answer my question, Joseph. Tell me what happened."

Potiphar looked at Joseph and again thought he saw sympathy in his face… or was it regret… or even apology? Joseph didn't answer. Potiphar's anger grew.

"Joseph," he said, the anger now clear in his voice, "if you don't answer my question, I will have no choice but to have you thrown into prison."

Still Joseph would not answer, and after one last attempt to wring an answer from him, Potiphar angrily left the room to fetch his guards. As captain of Pharaoh's guard and commander of the prison, Potiphar had no shortage of guards, and he soon returned with enough to arrest Joseph and take him down to the dungeons in which Pharaoh's prisoners were kept. These dungeons were famous throughout Egypt —everyone knew that most of the prisoners who entered "The Pit" never came out alive.

Potiphar accompanied the guards to the entrance to The Pit, where he met the officer who supervised the prison for him.

"Keeper of the prison," Potiphar greeted him, formally, "hold this man in prison."

"Yes, sir," replied the officer. "Is there any specific length of sentence, sir?"

"No," Potiphar snapped, irritably. "I will include all the necessary details when I send you the paperwork tomorrow."

"Very well, sir," acknowledged the man, looking awkward. "Ah, sir…. Where should the prisoner be kept and what privileges should he enjoy? I need to put him somewhere tonight, you see, so I can't really wait until the paperwork comes. I'm sorry, sir."

"It is a fair question, Ahmes," said Potiphar wearily. "He must go in The Pit, on one of the lower levels." Once more he turned and looked at Joseph, who was standing quietly in his chains, his face expressionless. Potiphar shook his head, and his anger dissipated completely. "But don't be too hard on him," he finished. Then he walked away.

Chapter 22

In The Pit

Potiphar delivered the paperwork the next day as promised, and Ahmes, the keeper of the prison, found that Joseph was to be remanded in custody indefinitely. There was normally little communication between the prison staff and the staff of Potiphar's household, but the keeper of the prison had heard something of Joseph before the summer evening when he was brought in by two guards as night was falling. Since the comments had all been good, Ahmes assumed that it was just another case of a clever but flawed individual overreaching himself and getting caught out.

He spoke to Joseph to find out what had happened, but received no response. No admissions, but no justification either. Simply silence. It was rather puzzling. The paperwork didn't help either, so Ahmes resorted to seeking out gossip from the servants in Potiphar's household. When he heard the reports, he was amazed that Joseph was still alive, and began to suspect that there must be more to this story than met the eye. Still, it was none of his business: he would just obey Potiphar's commands and keep the young man locked up.

Time passed, and, once again Joseph showed himself to be hard-working, reliable and trustworthy. But this time the confirmation was slow – excruciatingly slow. Shut up deep in The Pit, Joseph spent most of his time entirely alone. What a colossal change for one who had grown up with brothers everywhere, engulfed by the hustle and bustle of a large family encampment, rarely able to be alone even if he wanted to! Now, entire days were often spent with no human contact at all.

Silence became his close companion – silence and darkness. Yet it was not quite silence. Day after day, he strained to hear anything of the outside world, but the only sounds were from within: the occasional scuffle or squeak of the starved rats and other vermin that eked out a desperate existence among the putrid drains and stinking corridors that penetrated the lower levels of this fetid pile. The measured, tireless dripping that plucked at the fringes of his hearing made it worse. At times, he could hear it, faint but clear, its pitch as unchanging as the black darkness that surrounded him. Often he counted the drips for hours, his painful familiarity with its utterly consistent frequency allowing him to continue the count even when other noises interrupted. Yet at other times, he struggled to hear the sound at all, and the fear which had colonised the recesses of his mind spread its tendrils to overrun his waking thoughts. Was he becoming disconnected from the real world? Unimaginable relief flooded through him when once again he could hear the faint silvery dripping, like feathers that brushed against the farthest frontiers of his senses.

Through unmeasured time, his eyes sought light as a starving man seeks food, but there was no light to be seen, and the hopeless, endless search for it left him more desperate than ever; starting to see lights that weren't there.

Joseph struggled to hold on to his calm confidence – in fact, he struggled to hold on to his sanity – and without his faith in El Shaddai, he would never have succeeded.

But despite the almost unbearable loneliness, darkness and silence, there were still occasional opportunities: chances to help and opportunities to demonstrate patience and a willingness to work. Joseph took every one, because he was Joseph.

Food came only every second day in those dark recesses away from the ordinary world of time and space. The guards were used to prisoners who screamed at them or grabbed at them and refused to let go. Joseph welcomed his guards with a quiet acceptance of his situation and never complained. He showed gratitude for his food and helped with cleaning up the buckets that he must use for toileting.

Over time, the effect of his attitude on the guards was profound. It was happening again. Joseph would always rise to the top because of his attitude and the behaviour it engendered in him. Joseph really was different – outstanding; irresistible. Almost any other person consigned indefinitely to that black dungeon would have been broken, mind and body unable to cope with the terrible stress of solitary blackness.

℞

The heavy door swung slowly open and the light of a burning torch disturbed the blackness of Joseph's cell as two guards walked in.

"Food, Joseph," said the first.

"Ah, good. I'm hungry."

"Well you get better food than anyone else in this cell has ever received."

"I think the cook does a good job with my food, and I'm always eager to eat!"

A second guard, silent and watchful, carried the burning torch and was always ready with a sword. Yet even he had relaxed in his dealings with Joseph. He still never spoke, in fact he couldn't, but he did respond to

Joseph's friendly overtures as best he could, with nods and even the occasional smile.

"The cook put a special sweet something in your bowl today. You're getting spoiled, Joseph."

"Do you remember the wooden bucket you used to bring my food in?"

"I do. I changed it because it didn't seem fair. It was too filthy to clean up. I had to get permission for that."

"Thanks for your kindness. The food definitely tastes better in this bowl," said Joseph, smiling in the flickering torchlight.

"Oh, and about your meals, Joseph; Ahmes told me this morning that I am to feed you every day from now on. Wonders will never cease: feeding a prisoner in solitary every day!"

"Praise God! That's something to look forward to. But am I to stay in solitary forever?"

"It's orders. Direct from Potiphar, they were, and until they change, you'll stay here."

"Well, I can't expect Ahmes to go against his orders. How is my lord Potiphar, anyway? Do you see him or hear news about him?"

"Potiphar still has the favour of Pharaoh and manages his prisoners well. I believe he speaks to Ahmes often and everyone shows him great respect. I envy him his job, but I don't envy him his wife. But I know that you don't want me to talk about Zulaykha like that, so I won't. I just don't know how Potiphar can be so blind when it comes to the sorts of things she gets up to."

Joseph changed the subject and the discussion passed on to stories of the prison and other prisoners. Prisoners came and went, but many of those who went did so through the gate that led to the fires where the dead bodies were burned.

After a while, the guards left and Joseph's cell was plunged once more into darkness. The almost-silence returned as well, but Joseph had been given a morsel of hope. Food every day was something to look forward to, and the guards who delivered the food were company. It all helped to anchor his mind in reality. His circumstances were slowly improving.

Potiphar made occasional enquiries as part of his reviews of prisoners and was pleased to hear of the gradual improvement in his fortunes. Privately, he would still have liked to have adopted Joseph as his son, but it simply wasn't possible. A man cannot adopt as son a man whom his wife has accused of assault and attempted rape!

After Joseph had been in The Pit for almost four years, Zulaykha was caught in unfaithfulness with a young soldier. Enquiries showed that this was not the first such dalliance she had had, but that none had previously been reported to Potiphar out of consideration for his situation. Once again, it was the sympathy that roused his anger, and he quickly divorced Zulaykha and sent her back to her parents in shame. Of course, despite his suspicions, Potiphar could find no proof that she had fabricated the entire story about Joseph, so he could still do nothing significant to help him – not yet at least. But he did want to ease Joseph's suffering. Potiphar mulled over the possibilities, wondering even if adoption might still be an option, in time – after all, he was not getting any younger.

Anyway, thought Potiphar, it was best to start with small steps, and maybe he could do more later.

Potiphar gave the order, and Joseph's years of solitary confinement were over.

Joseph was moved from the lowest level of the prison up to a level where light again distinguished day from night. He was given a much more comfortable cell and considerable freedom within the prison. Slowly Ahmes, the keeper of the prison, began to use him as an extra staff member, almost another supervisor. Once again it had happened: Joseph had risen to the top.

But he was still in prison. Still the outside world beckoned, and still he longed for freedom; for the feel of the wind on his face, and the sound of his brother Benjamin's voice. Although he did not know it at the time, he had spent almost eleven years in Egypt, half of it in that dark pit – though he had done nothing that deserved such a punishment.

Sadly, Potiphar never had the opportunity to do any more for Joseph. One day, news came to the prison that an abscess beneath a tooth had spread poison throughout Potiphar's body, and Pharaoh was looking for a new leader of his guards. Joseph wondered what happened to slaves when their master died, but maybe no-one in the house above remembered him anymore. Potiphar had never come to see him in The Pit, and now he never would. Joseph felt sadness for the man who had been a kind master – until he had found himself in a position from which he could see no way out. Joseph had been just an expendable slave who must suffer to maintain peace in Potiphar's family – though in the end it hadn't worked anyway: Zulaykha's unfaithfulness had still caught her out.

So Potiphar was dead. Joseph mulled over the matter and decided that his time in Egypt must have been longer than he had believed. He had not been able to accurately keep track of his time in the lowest dungeon. Even as his situation had improved in The Pit, any attempt to reflect on that period brought him to a block in his memory, a time which his mind would not let him examine. All he could bring to mind was a frigid blackness and a sense of years unending.

He must find out how long he had been there. He would have to overcome his unwillingness to talk about that time and ask Ahmes how long he had languished in that dark hole struggling desperately to maintain his grasp on reality.

It took some time to work up the courage to broach the subject, and Ahmes' answer when it came both shocked him and confirmed his fears. *Four years* he had spent listening to that incessant dripping – or feeling terrified when he couldn't hear it. Four years submerged in squalor, waking terrified every night as nameless vermin scrabbled nearby or brushed against him in the blackness. The fear of that ever-present horror surged again, threatening to overwhelm him, and it was only his faith in the nearness and love of El Shaddai that allowed him to keep it under control – just as it had done through those days that seemed to have no end in his memory.

He did his best to put the memories behind him, recalling only the years of his life it had consumed. Yet he did not want to forget that God had brought him safely through that time. Without El Shaddai, he might even now be a gibbering madman, mouldering in the depths of The Pit.

Chapter 23

Special prisoners

One day, two special prisoners arrived along with orders from the new captain of Pharaoh's guard telling Ahmes to assign them to Joseph's particular care. Pleased that his positive reports about Joseph had been attended to by the new captain, Ahmes delivered the prisoners immediately to Joseph. Special prisoners required special care, and in Ahmes' opinion, Joseph was the best there was at giving special care. If a person needed someone to talk to, Joseph could discuss all sorts of helpful or encouraging subjects. If his companion needed silence, he would sit in companionable silence for as long as it took. And if it was best to just sit back and listen, he listened better than any other person Ahmes had ever met. Ahmes had even used Joseph in this way himself from time to time when the administrative requirements of his job became too much for a practical man to bear. And he wasn't too proud to undertake menial tasks either; no job of scrubbing or cleaning was beneath him. Joseph really was the answer to everything that any special prisoner might need. The only minor problem was his insistence that everything in the world revolved around his God. El Shaddai turned up in his conversation all the time, although the keeper of the prison had to admit that it always seemed to be in a wholesome and reasonable way – a way that somehow inspired appreciation and contentment. Funnily enough, that very fact made Ahmes actively seek Joseph out, and he spent many hours in conversation with this strange Hebrew slave.

Now, it has to be admitted that Pharaoh was a little erratic. At times his servants could make jokes and he would laugh and appreciate their humour, but in other moods, it was dangerous even to speak. However, silence could be dangerous too, and now Pharaoh's butler and baker had fallen foul of their master through silence.

Pharaoh had a strong conviction that Egypt was the greatest nation in the world. Comments on the greatness of Egypt were scattered frequently through his conversation, and he expected the same of his minions. Not only so, but he expected regular acknowledgement that Egypt's king was utterly without peer.

Any servant important enough to speak in the presence of Pharaoh must be clever enough to praise their lord and master frequently in ever new and genuine-sounding ways. Repeated or empty phrases were treated with suspicion, and it was on this point that Pharaoh's butler, Bebnum, and his baker, Kashta, had fallen short of expectations. Sparkling wit in devising new tributes to their lord's achievements had gained Bebnum and Kashta their respective positions, along with some ability in their fields of expertise. But recently, their eulogising had become less imaginative, even repetitive at times.

Pharaoh was deeply suspicious of people who seemed to ladle out praise as if it were broth – pleasant enough, but unexciting. Surely, he argued, if praise is genuine, it will not lapse into boredom or endless repetition. He was convinced that any servant whose praise of Egypt and its ruler was merely empty, unimaginative words could well be in the pay of a foreign power or plotting revolution against his lord.

And one morning when Pharaoh was sullen and irritable, Bebnum and Kashta had chosen the wrong time to maintain a cautious silence.

So here they were, dispatched to prison and a very uncertain future. Pharaoh might relent, or he might decide to dispose of them completely – or he might even forget about them altogether. This was one of the risks of working closely with Pharaoh. The butler and the baker were aware of this and were normally content with their lot, but not just then. Joseph didn't know it at the time, but he was to find out for himself just how much care was required in managing this most volatile of rulers.

Joseph arranged for the butler and the baker to be given a comfortable shared cell, where they would have time to think and to regret their mistakes, but not in a situation that would lead them to despair. He served them and forgot some of his own troubles in listening to theirs.

He was very easy to talk to, and Bebnum and Kashta found that he seemed to understand exactly how they felt and why. They were a little perplexed by his constant references to his God, but overall, they felt that his company and help were worth the cost of his emphasis on religion. At times, they even asked him more about his God, since he seemed to understand what he believed more clearly than most people ever did. Joseph was always eager to take these opportunities, and would speak about the love and power of his God for as long as they would listen. He spoke of promises, of miraculous births, of angels and of a hope for the future, and it whiled away some quite enjoyable hours, helping them to forget their condition.

But time was passing and the butler and the baker began to fret. Pharaoh must have forgotten about them, and clearly had no intention of restoring them to their positions. A new butler and a new baker must have been appointed by now, and what chance would they have of getting their old jobs back? Life became rather hopeless, and Joseph's skills of encouragement were taxed to the utmost.

Wistful stories of times spent in Pharaoh's court, enjoying the reflected glory of the king and his nobles, revelling in an importance by association – these were what Bebnum and Kashta dwelt on. But Joseph could see that their hopes were fading.

Then one night the butler had a dream. Next morning he was awake early, waiting eagerly for Joseph to attend them so that he could tell him about it. It had been a dream of the good old days. He had stood, holding Pharaoh's cup, in front of a vine with three branches loaded with buds, which had blossomed and developed into clusters of ripe grapes as he watched. He had eagerly squeezed the grapes, collecting their bountiful juice in Pharaoh's cup.

Joseph had hardly entered the room before the butler was telling him all about the dream, describing how he had finally been able to place the cup in Pharaoh's hand once more and bask in his smiling pleasure. But it had been no ordinary dream of the night that departed with the morning light. This dream felt different from those transient phantoms. The butler confessed that he was concerned because it felt as though the dream had a meaning, and he was worried what the meaning might be. "Joseph, do you know anything about interpreting dreams?" he asked anxiously.

Joseph smiled, remembering his dreams in Canaan and how obvious their interpretations had been. None of his hearers then had needed any explanation as to what those dreams had meant. But this dream was different, and Joseph took the time to think through all of its details: the branches, the buds and blossoms, the clusters of grapes, the juice pressed into Pharaoh's special cup – and the mysterious number three. He also took the time to pray for understanding, and as he did so, retelling the dream in his prayer, he felt an understanding of the dream seeping slowly into his mind. The wonder of this answer to prayer filled him to overflowing with thankfulness and humility, so he took a little extra time as well – time to thank the God who had no equal and yet had answered the prayer of an unimportant slave locked up in an Egyptian dungeon.

Bebnum, the butler, stood waiting for an answer for some moments, but when he saw Joseph falling into deep thought and meditation, he went and sat down in one of the chairs provided in this comfortable cell. Joseph was so absorbed that he didn't even seem to notice that the man had walked away. As the butler watched, various expressions passed across Joseph's face: concentration, uncertainty, and finally an unfolding, all-encompassing joy.

It was not until some minutes later that Joseph stirred and seemed again to become aware of his surroundings. "Your dream is rather simple, and my God has given me an understanding of it."

"Wonderful," said the butler, eagerly.

"Here is the interpretation," said Joseph. "The three branches are three days, and that is the key to the entire dream."

Everyone knew that it was Pharaoh's birthday in three days, and everyone knew about Pharaoh's birthday celebrations. The occasion was celebrated differently each year, but the parties were always grand and often showed the king's liberality to his servants.

"In three days," Joseph continued, "Pharaoh will raise you up again and restore you to your old job. You will again put Pharaoh's cup in his hand."

"Really?" asked the butler, looking joyful, but a little uncertain. "Are you sure?"

Joseph looked at him, and for a moment Bebnum felt a little like a doubting child being reproved by his parent. "I am certain," replied Joseph. "God's revelations of the future always come true. But when it comes true, please put in a good word for me with Pharaoh. I was sold in Egypt as a slave, although I had done no wrong, and now I am here in Pharaoh's prison, though I have done nothing to deserve being locked up in The Pit. Please talk to Pharaoh. He can release me."

Now it was Kashta's turn. He also had dreamed, but he had some doubt about his dream: it had seemed a little dark, as if it portended no good. However, the happy outcome of Bebnum's dream emboldened him to ask. Joseph was a good man and would surely give him a good interpretation.

"I too dreamed a dream," said the baker, a little cautiously. "I had three baskets of delicious cakes and other baked delights on my head. Although I couldn't see them, I knew that they were cooked to perfection. The top basket was full of particularly enticing baked goods for Pharaoh, but greedy birds kept flying down and pecking hungrily at them. It was heartbreaking, but I just couldn't stop it."

Once again, Joseph listened carefully, but this time he seemed to see the meaning immediately. The three baskets were three days, but for the one who dreamed it the meaning of the dream was terrible. Joseph prayed again for confirmation: was his understanding of the dream correct? All the details seemed to make sense, but he felt sorry for the baker, who was watching him with such eager anticipation. Could there be any other interpretation, or could the fulfilment be avoided? His prayer took time, and the baker paced back and forth across the cell as Joseph struggled. Finally Joseph was convinced that the dream was clear and its interpretation sure.

"Kashta, this dream is similar, but its interpretation will bring you no joy," Joseph said gently. "The three baskets are three days. In three days, Pharaoh will take you out of prison too, but he will hang you on a tree and the birds of the air will feed on you."

The baker looked utterly shattered, and his response showed his confidence in Joseph's interpretation. "But can't we do anything about it? How can I avoid it?" His voice was becoming increasingly shrill. "I don't deserve to die!"

Joseph did his best to calm the man, but he had no joy to offer him, only the certainty that God's word would be fulfilled. He did offer him one possible opportunity: worship God and pray for relief. But the baker was not a religious man, nor did he want to be. Life was for living, not for being constrained by the ridiculous rules of imagined gods.

"But this is not an imagined god," insisted Joseph. "This is the God who has interpreted these two dreams. When they are fulfilled, he will have proved that he is a great God, the only God who can interpret dreams and predict the future. If you wait until you have complete proof, it will be too late."

"I'll think it about," said the baker, but both he and Joseph knew that he had no intention of thinking any further.

Joseph pondered what he could do to make the man change his mind and think seriously before it was too late, but he had seen this attitude to religion before. He knew many people for whom life was life and death was death. No hope for the future was important or convincing enough for them to change their life now. They would not consider any genuine submission to God. Other gods could be honoured at the worshipper's convenience, certain rituals observed and everyone satisfied in a popular religion, but the God whom Joseph worshipped was not the same, and the way Joseph spoke of him to others showed that this was no religion of convenience. This was life and obedience.

Bebnum was overjoyed by the interpretation of his dream and began to dream his own dreams of a life returned to happiness. Immediately he began mentally to put his time in prison behind him, as a chapter that was almost closed. For Joseph it was satisfying to see the man's confidence in the words of God, but he still took the opportunity to repeat frequently that this knowledge of the future was from the God who had created everyone and everything. The butler listened politely, but was clearly preoccupied with his own hopes and plans.

The first day passed, and the baker changed his opinion. He completely rejected Joseph's interpretation of his dream and laughed off the dream itself as unimportant.

By the end of the second day, his professed doubts had infected the butler, who began to question Joseph's words and to lose his confidence that this time in prison would end well. He even began to speculate that he might receive an undeserved punishment from Pharaoh.

The third day came as a day of expectancy. According to the baker, there was nothing to worry about, no indication at all that anything would make this day different from any of the others in all the months they had stayed in The Pit – but he was nervous anyway.

Midday passed and still there was no sign of any action from Pharaoh. The baker began to feel a little happier and the butler's remaining optimism was taking a beating. Joseph remained quietly confident.

It was quite late in the afternoon when the keeper of the prison received an unexpected visit from an officer of Pharaoh, attended by six soldiers. He was carrying a folded sheet of papyrus with Pharaoh's seal attached and was accompanied by the captain of the guard. He too was carrying a piece of papyrus. "Ahmes," he said, "Pharaoh has sent to fetch two special prisoners: Bebnum, the former chief butler, and Kashta, the former chief baker. Here is the command from Pharaoh and here is the paperwork for releasing these men from prison. They are to be handed over to this officer and his soldiers so that they can be taken to Pharaoh immediately."

The captain of the guard handed over the prisoner release form to the keeper of the prison and left. Ahmes led the soldiers into the prison area where Joseph was arranging for one of the prisoners to receive medical treatment.

"Joseph," he called. "Which cell are Bebnum and Kashta kept in?"

"Cell 103," replied Joseph, "Do you want me to open it?"

"Yes," replied Ahmes. "Both prisoners are to be handed over to these soldiers, who will take them to Pharaoh. It's his birthday today and he is having a party for his servants. From what I hear, there will be both good news and bad news for these two."

"Have you heard what is happening to them then?" asked Joseph.

Ahmes looked at Pharaoh's officer questioningly.

"Not yet," said the officer, who still held the sealed sheet of papyrus. "Pharaoh doesn't want to let the cat out of the bag too early."

Joseph led the way to cell 103 and opened it with the keys he carried on his belt. Stepping back, he allowed the keeper of the prison to enter first, followed by the soldiers, and finally by Pharaoh's officer.

"Pharaoh has sent to fetch you," said Ahmes, and the faces of the two prisoners showed their shock. The first step of Joseph's interpretation of their dreams had come true. For Bebnum, this encouraged him to hope that the rest would follow, but for Kashta – the fear rose in his throat and his eyes widened in terror.

"What is going to happen to us?" asked Kashta anxiously. "Has Pharaoh decided to forgive us?"

"I can't say," replied Ahmes. "Pharaoh will tell you your fate when he thinks best."

"But we already know," wailed Kashta. "He told us!" – pointing to Joseph.

"How would he know?" asked Ahmes, looking confused.

"We each had a dream and he interpreted them for us. He told Bebnum that he would go back to his old job."

"And what about you?" asked the officer of Pharaoh. "What did he say about you?"

"He told me I was going to die," mumbled Kashta, "but I don't believe it."

"But there is no way he can know that!" replied the officer. "I don't even know myself. Pharaoh said that he hadn't told anyone."

All eyes were on Joseph, and he replied calmly, "Pharaoh didn't tell me. El Shaddai, the mighty God, told me. He knew it before even Pharaoh did."

"So mighty that he only talks to slaves, hey?" asked Kashta defiantly.

"Does he talk to you often?" asked Ahmes.

"No, he doesn't talk to me often," replied Joseph, still calmly, "but from time to time he makes me understand secrets and details of the future."

"Well, now we'll get to test your words," said Ahmes. "But first let's deal with the formalities. Bebnum and Kashta, I deliver you to these soldiers at Pharaoh's command as delivered to our lord, the captain of the guard."

Two guards stepped forward and grasped Bebnum by the arms. He willingly walked with them to the door.

"Don't forget to tell Pharaoh about me," said Joseph as the door was opened.

"Of course I won't," said Bebnum. "But first it's up to Pharaoh what he does with me. If things turn out as you said, I guarantee that I will tell Pharaoh about you."

Two more guards stepped forward to take Kashta by the arms, while a third stood in front of him with a drawn sword. Everyone in the room seemed to assume that Joseph's words would come true, and so the chief baker was being allowed no chance of escape.

Left alone in the cell, Joseph began to clean it up. He was sorry to say goodbye to the butler and the baker. They had brought him news from outside the prison and had been more pleasant company than many of the other prisoners he cared for. But he was particularly sorry for Kashta, whom he knew he would not meet again. Kashta had a wife and four sons, and who would care for them after he had been executed?

Joseph finished cleaning the cell and left, shutting the door behind him. The occupants wouldn't be back.

Chapter 24

Dreams fulfilled

The next day, news came that the butler had been brought before Pharaoh, who had complained bitterly about his new butler: the man had not understood how to give Pharaoh his drinks properly or how to mix them correctly. Not only that, but he had not known when to keep his mouth shut and leave Pharaoh in peace. As a result, he had been banished to his land in the south and Bebnum would regain his old position in Pharaoh's court. Pharaoh welcomed him back, but warned him to be careful not to upset him through a sombre silence or a critical attitude. Pharaoh wanted a happy throne room where personal and national achievements were acknowledged with wit and generosity. Of course, Bebnum must still make sure that he did not talk too much either!

Bebnum breathed a sigh of relief and took the warning to heart, deciding not to bring up the matter of Joseph immediately. Chattering immediately about a slave who could predict Pharaoh's actions might not be wise. The matter was not urgent.

Later that same evening, Kashta had also been called before Pharaoh, but now his mien was not encouraging. As the baker approached, he glanced up at Pharaoh's resentful face and a look of resignation spread across his own. When the soldiers stopped before Pharaoh, they let go of Kashta, but remained very close, ready to respond to any trouble. Kashta fell to his knees and bowed before Pharaoh with his face to the ground.

"Stand him up," said Pharaoh impatiently, and the soldiers took an arm each and dragged him upright. The wretched man tried to stand alone, but staggered and had to be supported by the soldiers. "I was angry with you for your sullen, boorish silence, but since you have been in prison I have also realised what a poor attitude you had to providing the king's food. The food you cooked looked much nicer than it tasted, and then at times you had the presumption to suggest that it was *my* taste that was at fault. I'm glad that I threw you into prison because now I have found a baker whose baked delights are beautiful to my eyes and taste even better than they look. As a baker, you are a failure, and as a servant of Pharaoh, you were insolent and insubordinate. We often had to put your baking out to be eaten by the birds, and now we will put you out to be eaten by the birds." Pharaoh waved his hand to the soldiers. "Take him out and hang him."

Kashta was dragged out, unable to walk and shaking in terror. Upsetting Pharaoh could be a fatal mistake.

☙

Joseph remained in The Pit, waiting patiently for the butler to arrange his freedom. At the start, it was easy to stay hopeful and explain why his freedom had not yet come, but as time went on, it became clear that freedom was not coming. There was no way to find out what had gone wrong; no way to contact the butler to remind him if the matter had just slipped his mind. Once again, Joseph had to get used to the idea that he was stuck in The Pit for an unspecified length of time. The little voice in the back of his head kept saying "Until you die", but his faith could not accept that.

In actual fact, what had happened was a sad combination of factors. Pharaoh's warning to the butler against talking too much had caused the latter to delay his mention of Joseph. After he had waited a while, although Joseph was still frequently on his mind, there were always reasons why he should not say anything to Pharaoh on that particular day: Pharaoh was not in a good mood, or the butler did not want to remind Pharaoh of the time when he had been angry with him. Then, as time passed, he thought of the matter less and less, and eventually Joseph was forgotten.

Two years passed in this way, the butler enjoying his revived fortunes and Joseph continuing to endure his undeserved suffering.

Joseph had endured the welcome of Egypt for thirteen years, and was only slowly recovering his peace of mind after the cruel torment in the darkness of The Pit.

He often thought of his home in the hours when he had little to do, once darkness had fallen and The Pit was locked up for the night.

He thought of his father and wondered if he was still alive. Or his grandfather Isaac – would he still be alive? He had been so very old, and even Great-grandfather Abraham had only lived to 175. Calculating ages, he worked out that Isaac would be 181 years old, and began to admit to himself that he would probably never see his grandfather again. And what of his brothers? Little Benjamin would be a teenager now if all had gone well. For all he knew, Benjamin might even be taller than he – maybe for all he would ever know. Reuben, Simeon, Levi and the others: what would they be like now? They had hated him and sold him as a slave, and he still remembered the dig made by the leader of the caravan as they had parted: "Maybe another of you will be for sale." He hoped that it had never come to that. Instead, he hoped that they had reformed their ways and sought paths of forgiveness and mercy – but he didn't know and maybe he never would. But he could never forget the dreams of his family bowing down to him. Did they speak of the future as the butler's and the baker's dreams had?

Chapter 25

Pharaoh's dreams

A night came when, for some reason he couldn't understand, Pharaoh dreamed two dreams and remembered them both. He woke in between and thought about the first dream for some time before falling asleep again and dreaming again.

This special night was to significantly change the future of at least two nations and many millions of people over thousands of years. And all because of a few vivid pictures in the mind of a restless monarch.

A forgetful butler would quickly be dragged into the embroidery of this complex, world-embracing tapestry, and a young Hebrew slave would suddenly find his life changed in ways that were impossible to imagine. As ripples spread out across a pool, so the situation would quickly spread to engulf the entire land of Egypt and, in just a few years, all of the surrounding nations. Then, in the centuries that followed, Egypt would turn a grateful family of welcome visitors into a nation of slaves who would finally escape Egypt only after a series of devastating plagues had wreaked vengeance on their overlords. The land promised to Abraham would be invaded by these escaping slaves, who would make it their own for almost a thousand years.

All this, then, from the strange dreams that filled Pharaoh's mind and troubled his sleep that night in his luxurious palace.

Bebnum, still chief cupbearer to the king, was one of the first to hear of these dreams. Immediately upon waking, Pharaoh had called for all the magicians and wise men in Egypt – all the people who could reasonably be expected to explain what were really two very strange dreams. Pharaoh could see clear similarities between them, but what they meant was beyond his comprehension.

Before him now were gathered all the magicians he could find, dressed in their finest clothes with embroidered pictures and eye-catching designs. Also present in the king's throne room were wise men who understood mathematics and geography, population dynamics and cultural diversity. All were waiting expectantly for guidance from Pharaoh. Such situations were worrying for these notables, but could also turn out to be wonderful opportunities for gaining even more fame and fortune.

The assembled men looked around at each other with jealous interest, noticing who was there and who was not, and therefore who their competition was in gaining the king's favour. Once everyone was present, Pharaoh waved his hand and asked for silence. He welcomed them all and described his requirements in just a few words. His cupbearer stood silently by his side, holding the king's cup, ready to give it to him should his voice begin to sound a little hoarse, or the cold he had been nursing cause it to fade a little.

So then, everyone now knew what was needed: an interpretation of Pharaoh's dreams. Surely that shouldn't be too difficult?

Pharaoh described his first dream to the attentive gathering, and all shared his satisfaction as seven healthy, plump cows came up out of the Nile River and fed in the reeds. But all likewise shared his disgust when seven gaunt, thin cows came out of the Nile too, and ate up the good cows.

Ideas for interpretations were whirling round in the minds of these wise men, but no one really liked the direction in which the dream seemed to tend. Surely the Nile River was Egypt itself, but if so, this was a message that worked against the glory of Egypt. Whatever it meant, it seemed to end badly. Was anyone willing to deliver that sort of a message to Pharaoh?

Wisely, the group agreed together that it was best to hear both dreams before giving the interpretation of either.

Pharaoh sipped a little wine from the cup Bebnum offered him, then began to describe his second dream. He had seen seven good, fat ears of corn growing on one stalk, just the sort of superb agricultural produce that one would expect in Egypt – but then another seven ears of corn had come up on the same stalk, thin and dried up by the hot east wind, ears such as were never seen before in Egypt for their shrivelled worthlessness. Yet these seven proceeded to eat the seven fat and good ears.

That was all there was to tell. After that, Pharaoh had woken again and wondered, but he had remained completely at a loss as to what the dreams might mean.

The two dreams were so similar in their essence that it would be a brave magician indeed who would suggest two different meanings. But if the Nile and the stalk were both Egypt, the dreams spelled disaster for the nation.

Wise man looked at wise man, and their wisdom tied their tongues. Magician looked at magician, and their cunning brushed off the idea of offering such an explanation to Pharaoh. Stories got around – although not always with complete accuracy – and prudent men feared anyone who could execute his chief baker for burning the cakes!

"What do my dreams mean?" asked Pharaoh, and sat back to await the answer.

He had to wait quite a while before anyone spoke, and even then it was only a wise man tentatively suggesting that these might just be run-of-the-mill, ordinary dreams such as everyone had from time to time; dreams with no particular significance.

Pharaoh looked at the wise man impatiently and dismissed the idea in just a few words: "Ridiculous. These dreams were far too real, far too similar, far too vivid and far too… I don't know quite how to put it, but… full of meaning!"

By now, everyone in the room was feeling uncomfortable – and worried. Pharaoh was not going to take No for an answer, but none of the magicians or wise men were foolish enough to give him the obvious answers.

Pharaoh told the story of his dreams one more time, just in case his experts had misheard or misunderstood, but he received no better response.

Finally, the cupbearer showed real bravery. His memory had been stirred by these references to dreams, and now he plucked up his courage to tell Pharaoh about Joseph. He even included the worrying detail of Pharaoh's anger, as well as his personal failure in not telling Pharaoh of Joseph's plight.

Pharaoh remembered the events well and was intrigued to hear that there was a slave in his own prison who had known what he was going to do before he told anyone.

"Guards, bring this Hebrew to me immediately."

Chapter 26

Surprises

The guards rushed off immediately to find this amazing interpreter of dreams, but fetching him took a little longer than Pharaoh might have anticipated. The new captain of the guard took them quickly to the keeper of the prison and the keeper of the prison took them straight away to Joseph, but when they saw him they were horrified. They could not possibly present this dirty, unshaven foreigner in rough, uncultured clothes before Pharaoh! So Joseph was sent to wash and shave and change his clothes. And hurry!

Hurry with the washing and hurry with the shaving. Hurry with the special clothes, brought by the messengers of the king. At least someone had realised that a slave who was a prisoner in The Pit was unlikely have any clothes formal enough to grace the king's throne room!

No time to think. No time for any detailed explanation. All Joseph knew as he walked toward the palace was that Pharaoh had had some dreams and needed interpretations.

Joseph had spent many years within easy walking distance of this palace, but now he entered it for the first time, hurried along by worried servants of Pharaoh.

"Quickly," they said, both separately and in unison – but above all, frequently. It was eight years since Joseph had last walked in the open air, and it smelled strange to him. Such a long time since this son of shepherds, raised to tend flocks, had seen the sky and felt the fresh breeze. Eight years!

But there was no time to think about that – the pressure was too great. If he couldn't satisfy Pharaoh's demands, would he not end up like the chief baker?

Pharaoh's servants watched Joseph with surprise as he walked into the palace with a look almost of calmness on his face. They hoped he would perform as the chief butler had suggested he could, because otherwise things would not go well for him or anyone else. When Pharaoh got a bee in his bonnet, it was dangerous for everyone.

Joseph was led rapidly to the massive doors that separated Pharaoh's throne room from the rest of the palace. These doors were made of thick timber, hung on massive hinges and decorated all over with valuable metals. The guards stopped before the doors and awaited the signal to enter. For most people, it would have been a time of unsustainable stress, but Joseph maintained his composure. In just a few moments, he would be brought into the throne room to face a king who was probably the most powerful man in the world, and expected to answer questions none of the experts could answer. Joseph had never stood in front of a king before, never had to present the correct appearance in keeping with the expectations of a royal court. Such niceties were completely foreign to him, a tent-dweller born and bred, yet they would be the first points on which he would be judged. Appearances are important for credibility, particularly when you can have no proof for the advice you offer. Dreams are tenuous things, and belief in any proffered interpretation will be fragile and elusive. Success for Joseph would depend as much on how he presented himself as on what he said – at least for the time being.

The future would judge the interpretations he presented, but for the time being, he must convince Pharaoh with nothing but his voice and charisma.

Fortunately, charisma was something that Joseph had plenty of, despite his general humility. When he entered a room, voices would often hush, and people sought his opinions more often than his position in life suggested that they should.

So it was in Pharaoh's throne room. As the doors opened slowly before them, Joseph was called forward and led towards Pharaoh as he sat on his golden throne. Slowly and serenely he approached Pharaoh, and the monarch was impressed by the confident appearance and easy bearing of this slave upon whom so much depended.

"Is this the slave you spoke of?" he asked Bebnum.

"Yes, your majesty."

"Slave," said Pharaoh, "come here and stand before me."

Joseph advanced obediently, flanked by cautious soldiers who watched him very carefully. Though focussing on Pharaoh, Joseph still gained the impression of a large room almost filled with people who were all staring at him. The magicians and wise men were still waiting at the king's command and appeared fascinated by this young-looking slave who seemed to radiate reliability.

Pharaoh continued, "My chief butler here has told me that you can interpret dreams. Now I have had a dream – two actually – and I need to know what they mean. None of my experts here," and Pharaoh sort of leaned a little on that word "experts" as he looked around at his magicians and wise men, "have been able to explain the dreams. I have heard that all you need to do is to hear a dream to be able to interpret it."

Joseph looked at Bebnum as Pharaoh gestured toward him, and saw the man's mostly impassive face soften a little to give a small smile that was probably intended to be encouraging. In fact, Bebnum was a worried man. He had felt compelled to mention Joseph, but believed it was a great risk to recommend this slave to Pharaoh. However, such was the effect that Joseph had on people, that Bebnum was reassured by that brief look from Joseph.

Pharaoh leaned back on his throne and waited for Joseph to explain his qualifications, but Joseph's actual words came as quite a surprise to him.

"It is not in me; God will give Pharaoh a favourable answer."

Pharaoh was surprised by his brevity and lack of flattery, but decided to reserve judgement. If this man really could give him the answers he needed through the power of his god, well and good – but he sounded a bit of a religious crank. Nevertheless, he began to describe his dreams, which he was now firmly convinced were just one dream anyway. The connections seemed to make it obvious.

"In my dream I was standing on the banks of the Nile. Seven cows, plump and attractive, just the sort of cows we normally have in Egypt, came up out of the Nile and fed in the reed grass." He stopped and bit his lip before continuing, "Then seven other cows came up after them, poor and very ugly and thin, such as I had never seen in all the land of Egypt. And those horribly thin, ugly cows ate up the first seven plump cows, but when they had eaten them no one would have known that they had done so, for they were still as ugly as at the beginning."

Joseph watched Pharaoh carefully as the story progressed, nodding from time to time.

"That's how it was," said Pharaoh. "Then I awoke."

Joseph appeared to think deeply and didn't seem in any hurry to answer. The magicians and wise men began to shift nervously. They would never have been willing to stand so long without making any response to the king, who was so clearly awaiting one.

Finally Joseph seemed about to speak, when suddenly Pharaoh held up his hand and continued the tale with his second dream.

"I also saw in my dream seven ears growing on one stalk, full and good, just as we would expect to grow in Egypt with the magnificent soil and the agricultural expertise so many of our farmers possess." He stopped and looked more doubtful again as he said, "Then seven more ears, withered, thin, and blighted by the east wind, sprouted after them, and the thin ears swallowed up the seven good ears. And I told it to the magicians, but there was no one who could explain it to me."

Joseph looked around in surprise at the waiting men, wondering why none would have had any suggestions as to what the dream might mean. The basic connection with Egypt seemed rather obvious. Could it be that God had kept them from seeing it, or was there something else? Were they afraid to follow the link between Egypt and the bad cows or shrivelled ears? He couldn't be sure, but that seemed the most likely explanation. If that really was the reason, then they must have cause for their fear. He had heard of Pharaoh's irritability… and then suddenly he understood. The chief butler and the chief baker had ended up in prison – and the baker had later lost his life – due to what seemed trivial offences. These magicians and wise men were probably afraid to upset Pharaoh with any negative reflection on Egypt and its agriculture.

He would have to be very careful and very positive or the gift of understanding that God had given him would be wasted.

Joseph prayed silently, expressing his grateful thanks to God for not only giving him understanding of the dream, but also showing him the importance of how he presented the interpretation to Pharaoh.

He saw clearly that understanding the dream was not all that would be required. He would need to have a watertight plan to present to Pharaoh, and as he thought about this, he began to see the plan unfolding in his mind's eye. He pictured Egypt gathering vast quantities of food and storing them against a time of famine. It was as if God was giving him a vision to show how the understanding of Pharaoh's dreams could lead to the saving of a nation.

Joseph was filled with a sudden certainty that the interpretation was right and the plan he had been shown was the very best plan possible. A feeling of utter wonder grew within him and he smiled widely at Pharaoh.

Pharaoh waited expectantly, but once again, Joseph first took the time to offer another quick prayer of thanks that now all the tools he needed to satisfy Pharaoh's demands had been placed directly into his hands.

Slowly, then, Joseph answered Pharaoh. Looking deep into Pharaoh's eyes, he spoke with a confidence which was easy to command because it was completely genuine.

"The dreams of Pharaoh are one; God has revealed to Pharaoh what he is about to do. The seven good cows are seven years, and the seven good ears are seven years; the dreams are one. The seven lean and ugly cows, and the seven empty ears blighted by the east wind, are also seven years – years of famine. It is as I told Pharaoh; God has shown Pharaoh what he is about to do."

Joseph specifically emphasised the work of God for Pharaoh to make sure that he himself was not given the praise. A lesser man, desperate to escape from unjust imprisonment, might have allowed a little of that praise to accrue to him, but that was not Joseph's way. About 1,700 years later, another man would come who would likewise make sure that he always directed all praise to God, but that example was not yet known. Joseph made this choice by himself, and had made it so much a part of himself that it was impossible to tell whether it was natural or learned.

Pharaoh was catching on to the meaning, but he wanted more detail.

Joseph continued to explain, "There will come seven years of great plenty throughout all the land of Egypt, but after them there will arise seven years of famine, and all the plenty will be forgotten in the land of Egypt because the famine will be so bad. The famine will consume the land because it will be very severe."

By this time, Pharaoh was nodding his head and leaning forward with conviction. The most dangerous part of delivering the interpretation was over – the confidence that God had given Joseph had carried the day. Nevertheless, Joseph must still explain the plan convincingly. It must not be allowed to fail.

"Pharaoh's dream was doubled because the thing is fixed by God, and God will shortly bring it about," he added, wanting to make it clear that preparations must begin immediately. He then proceeded urgently, "Now therefore let Pharaoh choose a discerning and wise man, and put him over all the land of Egypt. Let Pharaoh proceed to appoint overseers over the land and take one-fifth of the produce of the land of Egypt during the seven plentiful years. And let them gather all the food of these good years that are coming and store up grain under the authority of Pharaoh for food in the cities, and let them keep it. That food shall be a reserve for the land against the seven years of famine that are to come on the land of Egypt, so that the land may not perish through the famine."

Suddenly there was a spontaneous cheer in the throne room. The magicians and wise men were honestly delighted at seeing such a skilful and utterly convincing performance of their craft. In that, too, Joseph was like the great speaker who would follow him so many centuries later.

Pharaoh and Joseph both looked around in surprise, but then a smile bloomed on Pharaoh's face and he surveyed the room with pleasure. Standing up quickly, he moved unexpectedly towards Joseph and gave him a hug that surprised everyone, not least Pharaoh himself. He was very impressed by the demeanour of this young slave, and his suggestion that they should stockpile some of the bounty of the coming good years struck him as a stroke of genius.

He put his hand on Joseph's arm and beamed around at the assembled throng, saying, "Can we find a man like this, in whom is the Spirit of God?" A chorus of Noes echoed around the room, and Pharaoh looked pleased. He took Joseph by the arm and led him over to his throne, saying to a servant, "Bring a chair for…"

"Joseph," responded Joseph.

"Yes, for Joseph," said Pharaoh. "That will become a very famous name, I'm sure."

The servant placed a small chair near Pharaoh's throne and stepped back.

"Come and sit near me," said Pharaoh, sitting down again on his throne. Joseph sat down obediently, and Pharaoh said to him, "Since God has shown you all this, there is none so discerning and wise as you are. You shall be over my house, and all my people shall order themselves as you command. Only as regards the throne will I be greater than you."

Joseph wondered quietly to himself if such a change had ever happened in the world before. Had a slave ever been whisked from a dungeon and immediately become the second in command in the kingdom? Was this really happening or was it all just a dream?

"See, I have set you over all the land of Egypt," said Pharaoh, still smiling. Then Pharaoh took the signet ring from his hand and put it on Joseph's. Holding up Joseph's hand, he showed it to all the wise men and magicians.

"Joseph is second only to me in the kingdom, because he could interpret dreams when none of my 'experts' had any idea what to do. All of you magicians and wise men can leave. Joseph is all I need."

The magicians and wise men seemed less pleased with this announcement than they had been with Joseph's announcement of the meaning of the dream and the best solution to the problems it presented. However, they filed out anyway, and Joseph was left almost alone with Pharaoh.

Of course, there were still plenty of servants around, and on Pharaoh's orders, they took Joseph away and clothed him in garments of the finest linen.

When Joseph returned to the throne room shortly afterward, he found Pharaoh waiting for him with a heavy gold chain which was put about his neck by the hands of Pharaoh himself.

Chapter 27

Number Two

Life had changed again for Joseph. His life had seen some amazing ups and terrible downs. From favourite son to slave, to overseer in Potiphar's household, to prisoner – and now he was second in command of all Egypt. At last he was to begin the work that would save his family.

That night, he was given a comfortable room in one wing of Pharaoh's palace and left completely without interruptions. He was so unaccustomed to such comfort that he slept only fitfully, and used many of the hours of darkness working out what to do first in his new job.

The very next day, Pharaoh arranged a house for his new deputy, and Joseph found himself in a large house with an army of servants answerable to him. Not only so, but his new house was arranged in such a way that he could begin work immediately, preparing for the good years which God had said were coming soon.

And Joseph was ready to begin. His wakeful night had not been wasted, and he already knew many questions for which he needed answers. How much wheat, barley and other grain was grown in Egypt each year? What storage areas were available and how much grain could be stored in each? Were they secure? Could stored grain survive for 10 to 15 years, or would it all go mouldy or be eaten by rats?

Many questions about planning, costs and construction had also occurred to his astute mind, and after a little prompting, Pharaoh made sure that engineers and economists were standing by ready to answer his questions.

Of course, the more questions they answered, the more questions he had. He may have been appointed second in command, but he felt rather uninformed when it came to any technical questions. How much grain would he be collecting, and how many storage units would be necessary to store it? Where should the new storage areas be constructed to facilitate collection and safe storage of the grain, as well as easy distribution once the years of famine came?

Every day for weeks, Joseph had experts continually feeding him information about Egypt, so that when the bumper crops began there would be places prepared for storing the excess.

Joseph wasn't aware of it, but many of these experts had been required to provide reports to Pharaoh of what Joseph was talking to them about. Pharaoh wouldn't necessarily have given up on Joseph if he had found that his star recruit was floundering, but he wanted to be prepared just in case. Instead, he found that his experts were universally impressed with this ignorant foreign slave who seemed to know not only what questions to ask, but also how to use the answers he received. They were all amazed and Pharaoh was suitably satisfied.

From the reports of his experts, Pharaoh guessed that Joseph would soon begin travelling all over Egypt looking for suitable locations to build silos, so he gave Joseph his second chariot with its beautiful horses. Speed would be of the essence, so runners were appointed to run before him calling out, "Bow the knee!" Pharaoh rapidly found that Joseph wasn't interested in having people bow the knee, but that he was content to allow it to continue if it got them out of the way more quickly.

Joseph's fame and the effects of his plans began to spread all over Egypt. Pharaoh helped this along by giving him the ancient name "Zaphenath-paneah". This name had a few possible meanings, and all of them were superlatives: "Saviour of the World" some said it meant, while others said "Creator of Life", and still others suggested that it referred to Joseph being the mouthpiece of God, or a Revealer of Secrets. Whatever the name had meant originally, it was clear that Pharaoh had chosen it to praise the new workaday leader of Egypt.

Maintaining such a pace of enquiry and planning was not cheap, but Joseph did not begin the really expensive phase of the work until the evidence was there to place before Pharaoh. The very next growing season showed phenomenal promise. Seeds were planted only to explode into growth and produce vast quantities of grain. As soon as the evidence was available to confirm Pharaoh's faith in him, Joseph began the work that would cost the truly huge amounts of money. Silos were planned in every town, and the construction work would keep many Egyptians and slaves busy. It would also drain Pharaoh's coffers at a great rate. Yet that was only the beginning. Once the silos had been built, they had to be filled, and that meant buying grain in such quantities as most economists had never even contemplated.

Fortunately, the amazing fertility and superb growing conditions yielded so much grain that there was far more grain than there was demand. In the contradiction that is agriculture, the best years are typically rewarded with the lowest prices, so that bumper crops rarely earn the income a farmer would hope for.

Yields were up by 50 percent on a typical good year, which meant four or five times the harvest of an ordinary year where Egypt could produce all the grain it needed.

Joseph's target of collecting one fifth of these glorious crops left plenty for any other demand, and the prices plummeted. Farmers were overjoyed to receive the extra money from the government collection funds to bump up their income.

When the harvest of that first year of massive crops began to come in, Pharaoh rewarded Joseph in a most satisfying way: he gave him a wife, a helper and companion, and Joseph rejoiced. Asenath was the daughter of Potiphera priest of On, the city of the sun.

Joseph was slowly winning more and more of his heart's desires. He was free and had been given an opportunity to make sure that God's warnings would be heeded. The first of the expected seven years of massive crops was going as predicted, and Joseph's plans were falling into place.

This former Hebrew slave was just 30 years old, yet represented Pharaoh in everything that happened in Egypt. And Pharaoh was delighted. Everything that Joseph did turned out well, and there could be no question that he wanted everyone to know that this success came from his God. Joseph was always eager to tell people about the God who had shown him all he needed to know and cared for his family through centuries. Joseph was an excellent ambassador for God.

Busy though both were, Pharaoh slowly got to know his second in command and knew that, unfortunately, not everything was perfect for Joseph. Joseph longed for home and for his family, but at least the lovely Asenath was able to help assuage the longing somewhat when she delivered Joseph's firstborn son. He gave the boy the name "Manasseh", explaining to her that the name reflected the happiness they had together, in that God had made him forget all of his hardship and all of his family.

However, Asenath also knew that it was not entirely true and that Joseph still longed for his family, and might even have gone searching for them if he had not felt so keenly the responsibility of caring for his adopted land.

Time passed and the good years accumulated. More and more silos were built and the people increasingly took the astonishing bounty for granted.

For the first two or three years, many of the farmers kept a private store of grain from the surplus that filled their fields and barns to bursting. But as the good years kept coming, many started to feel that it was an unnecessary effort and not likely to be worth continuing. After all, Zaphenath-paneah, the saviour of Egypt, was collecting all they would need, so why not get some additional money from selling the extra?

Joseph did his best to discourage this attitude, but failed. It was almost the only area in which he did so.

Silos filled. New silos were built and they too were filled almost as soon as they were finished. Grain was stored all over Egypt, and the records carefully kept by Joseph confirmed that there was going to be enough seed to feed Egypt through the disastrous years that were coming.

Once again, Joseph and Asenath were blessed by the hand of God with the birth of another child. Joseph named him Ephraim, explaining to Asenath that the name meant "fruitful" in his native language. Asenath liked the name, as she liked everything that Joseph did or said. Her husband was the most admired man in all Egypt and she was very proud of him. She did wish that she could smooth away the furrows in his brow that came whenever he thought of his family in Canaan, but sadness of the heart is difficult to smooth away. Not even time can remove such sorrow completely.

Five good years, then six and finally seven passed by. Joseph faithfully collected every kernel of grain he could, until all of the silos were filled to overflowing. The original storage areas had already held their bounty for six full years, and the careful preparation showed in the quality of the seed after all that time. Of course, rats had been doing their best to help themselves, but even they had been affected by the overflowing supplies of seed and had seemed a little lethargic in seeking out ways to share in the earth's beneficence.

Now the focus must change.

From being an organisation that collected, constantly and extravagantly, Joseph's grain-gatherers must now develop a mechanism for distributing the abundance.

Pharaoh had paid for the collection of this vast sea of grain, and now he must recover his costs. Many thousands, possibly even hundreds of thousands, of people had collected tirelessly, and Pharaoh had paid their wages. Now they would be selling the grain to Pharaoh's people, earning their keep as the need grew. And it was Joseph who made all the plans and thought through all of the possible problems.

The harvests of the seventh year were barely gathered in when the farmers sensed a change in the weather. The winds grew stronger and dust filled the air much of the time. The water flowing down the Nile seemed to slow and almost curdle. Sluggish, mud-filled water struggled down the paths to the sea, and hard-working farmers found it more and more difficult to raise the water needed for their fields. No rain fell, even in the areas around the Nile where some rain was wont to fall every year. It didn't take long before people were acknowledging that Joseph had been in the right of it. The coming harvest wasn't looking good. Even the experts acknowledged the obvious and reduced their estimated yields, inflated by so many years of abundance.

"It's amazing," said one of Joseph's deputies, named Didia. "You certainly got it right, Zaphenath-paneah. Quite an amazing coincidence, when all is said and done."

"It is no coincidence, Didia, it is the hand of El Shaddai, God of the Hebrews. Just as I told you when you came to work for me. Didn't you believe me?"

"Well," replied Didia, carefully, "it's clearly happening, but the gods don't just do what we want when we tell them."

"I never said it was because of what *I* wanted," said Joseph. "God made the decision, God gave the message in Pharaoh's dream, and then God gave me the understanding I needed to see his truth. This is not us telling God, it is God telling us."

Pharaoh was satisfied that his faith in Joseph was being repaid. Drought and famine were coming right on schedule. He just hoped that Joseph's plan for the time of famine would work as well as his plan for the time of plenty had done.

Chapter 28

Famine

Hot, dry days were followed by hot, dry nights, and the seed that was sown gradually shrivelled and died, then blew away on the winds.

Happy and expectant farmers for whom work had become easy were reawakened to reality with a rude shock. Growing crops was no longer as simple as putting seeds in the ground and then stepping back to watch them flourish, outgrowing the weeds with little effort. Farming was back to being drudgery at its worst, where even hard work was not rewarded.

Some farmers had no crops at all that year. Many farmers grew less than they had sown, and only a few had crops that were worth reaping. With one accord, they threw up their hands and complained.

The famine had come as a nasty shock to most of the farmers.

This may seem unbelievable given that Joseph had announced the expected weather patterns extensively over the previous seven years, but very few had actually believed him. Farmers know that weather is unpredictable and that, if the gods are truly in control, they must be very fickle and arbitrary. Making consistent offerings keeps the priests happy, but seems to have no consistent effect on the weather. So when Joseph and his men announced that there would be seven good years followed by seven bad years, the information didn't make it past the farmers' listening filters. They simply ignored it. Of course, they were pleased when the good years came, but few ever made the connection between the good harvests and Joseph's predictions.

Some recognised the famine and suggested that the gods of Egypt were angry and must be appeased. Others just complained – as is the habit of those who live off the land. When there is nothing that can be done, there is a certain fellowship in complaining together.

At the end of the last good year, Joseph had travelled around to all of his collection points and carried out thorough inspections, insisting that his men take particular care to check that all the silos were secure. Rats, birds, insects and people would all come looking for food, and the stockpiled grain must not be allowed to be lost so easily. Detailed records were compiled and the stewards of the stored grain were made to understand that it was precious and must not be squandered through carelessness. A complete accounting would be required for all the grain in each silo – Pharaoh's money must be recouped.

Joseph had been acutely aware of the strangeness of speaking of drought and famine when the land was lush and green and seemingly never-ending rivers of grain were still pouring into Pharaoh's innumerable silos. It would be easy for the silo managers to take life easy and lose the advantage careful planning had gained.

Before long, the small stores of grain that individuals had laid aside were all used up. Everyone had seen the wonderful harvests and Pharaoh's vast stores and decided that they had no need to collect for themselves. It may have been a reasonable conclusion, but it was to cost them dearly.

No grain means no bread, and soon there was a cry for bread throughout the length and breadth of Egypt. There were even a few isolated attacks on Pharaoh's silos, mostly by hostile individuals.

Pharaoh directed the population to Joseph, and Joseph opened the storehouses and began selling grain to any who came. The nations around Egypt were suffering from the same famine, and as the news spread, many starving foreigners also came to Egypt to buy grain from Joseph.

One year of famine had passed. Six long, weary years were still to come.

⸎

"Joseph, do you think your family is still alive?" asked Asenath.

"I don't know," responded Joseph glumly. "There are many things that can go wrong in the world and it's 21 years now since I last saw them. I think that some must be alive, because God's promises to Great-grandfather Abraham must be fulfilled – through Isaac, Abraham will have as many descendants as there are stars in the sky. I still look at the stars often and remember his promises. But then again, since I am alive, I suppose I can't be sure of the others. Maybe the promises will be fulfilled through you and me, through Manasseh and Ephraim."

"Would they come to Egypt to get grain if they needed it, Joseph? You have spoken of people coming from many nations to get grain. Do you think your family might come?"

"I had hoped that they would, but if they were going to come, I would have expected them during the last year," replied Joseph sadly. "That's one of the reasons why I made the rule that all foreigners had to come to this central location to purchase grain. Egyptians can go to their nearest silo, but foreigners must come here. That way, I knew I wouldn't miss them if they came. So unless someone has sold them grain from another silo, they haven't come."

"But they still might come."

"Yes, they might," Joseph agreed, and sighed. "They might be coming even now – or they might all be dead. I just don't know. That is why it's all so difficult to cope with."

Asenath laid her hand on his and looked at him with sympathy in her beautiful eyes. Joseph didn't think that she looked much like his mother Rachel, although both were beautiful, but sometimes she reminded him of her. Joseph particularly remembered his mother for her courage and faithfulness. Although he did not realise it, these were two characteristics he had inherited from her, along with a determination to keep going when times were tough. From his father had come his skill with planning and his uncanny knack of knowing what others were thinking. But his strong spirituality, his closeness to God, had come from both parents, and had been constantly practised and sharpened at every turn by Joseph himself.

He looked wistfully at Asenath, appreciating her beauty and the kindness that suited her so well. As he had done so many times before, he gave thanks to God that he had been able to resist the seductions of Zulaykha and maintain the faithfulness that was so important both to him and to the God he worshipped. How different life would have been if he had given in. How long would it have been before she had tired of him and cast him off like an old rag? And then what false report would she have concocted to get him into trouble? Poor Potiphar. He had been a good master, but what a burden of a wife to carry!

He dragged his thoughts back to the present, smiled at Asenath and said, "Don't worry about me. El Shaddai is in control, whether he sent me here to be the only survivor of my family or the one who could help the rest of his family survive. I just can't tell yet which it is."

"What about those dreams you told me about?" asked Asenath. "The ones about your brothers bowing down to you, and your mother and father as well."

"Yes, I think those will have to be fulfilled – unless they were just conceited nonsense from my own ego. Can I really be sure that they were dreams from God that foretold the future?"

"I've never met anyone with less of an ego than you, Joseph," replied Asenath, smiling. "And I wouldn't tell you that if it wasn't true – otherwise it would swell your head too much!"

Joseph laughed, and responded, "Oh, no, Asenath, I have ego enough and to spare! But when I think that any ability I have comes only from El Shaddai anyway, it stops me thinking that I deserve praise for the things he helps me do. After all, where would I be without him? Dried bones at the bottom of a pit in Canaan? A dead slave in The Pit?"

"You're right, but sometimes your God doesn't work as quickly as one might hope."

"That's because I'm a slow learner. That's just how long it took to make me the man that God could use to help Pharaoh. I couldn't have done it without either the joys or the suffering. And you couldn't complain about how quickly he moved me from The Pit to the palace, could you?"

"No – in fact, I can't complain about any of it, if that's what it took to make you what you are. I am very blessed to have you as my husband. You have taught me so much.

I would never have known about El Shaddai without you."

"I'm not so sure that your father wanted you to learn about El Shaddai," replied Joseph, drily.

"I'm sure you're right," she said, smiling again, "but I'm glad that I did."

"But even you didn't seem very pleased with my God when I first met you."

"I suppose not, but that was because my father had told me that you had dishonoured the gods of Egypt by your interpretation of Pharaoh's dreams. But it didn't take me long to see that your God was much better than the gods of Egypt."

"And it didn't take me long to realise that it was very important for you to know about El Shaddai, and to worship him."

"My father said that you watched me everywhere I went that day, and that it was very obvious to everybody, including Pharaoh."

"I had never seen anyone so beautiful in all my life," he said simply. "But that wasn't all, as you know. It was the way you talked and thought too."

"It was very flattering to have Pharaoh's deputy talk to me all afternoon, even if he did speak of nothing but wheat and barley and storehouses."

"I didn't know what to talk about – I couldn't look at you and *think* at the same time! I still can't."

"After a while, though," she said with a twinkle, "you started to answer my questions about your life and your hopes, and then you seemed to be able to think."

"Yes, a bit – but that was when I upset your father and mother by talking about El Shaddai and what he had done for my family. If I had really been thinking, I might not have done that. It might have stopped us from getting married at all if Pharaoh hadn't stepped in."

"True, but I found it fascinating all the same. I had never heard of a god who could be so close and personal. When I compare your God with the trivial, empty gods of Egypt, I don't want to have anything to do with them. And yet they are the gods my father is priest of."

"I suppose it's all about whether you want a cruel, impersonal god, or even one that you can shape to your own ways; or whether you choose to acknowledge a god who tries to shape *you* to *his* ways. Particularly when you find that his ways are the embodiment of kindness and generosity."

"You have certainly learned kindness and generosity, my husband," Asenath said, looking at him with love.

"And you have helped to teach me those things as well as many others, Asenath… what are you laughing about?"

"Well, I've heard you say before that we only really learn things through suffering," she gurgled. "Is that what you mean? That you have to suffer me?"

They shared a happy laugh together and were still laughing when five-year-old Manasseh walked in, struggling to carry his younger brother, a chubby, happy, 18-month-old infant.

"Down!" said Ephraim, wriggling.

"No," replied Manasseh, "I have to look after you."

"Down!" repeated Ephraim, starting to squirm more vigorously than before.

Manasseh put him down with more haste than control and asked eagerly, "Do I have any cousins? Amenmose has cousins." Amenmose was a servant who looked after the cooking staff, but he liked Manasseh and Ephraim and often played with them.

"You know that my brother has three sons," said Asenath. "They are your cousins."

"Yes, but I meant Daddy's relatives. Daddy had lots of brothers, didn't he?"

"Yes, I had lots of brothers, and I may still have lots of brothers – I just don't know," Joseph replied.

"Do any of your brothers have boys like me?" asked Manasseh.

"I don't know much about who has what, now," answered Joseph. "But when I left, my brother Judah had three sons and Asher had one son, so I suppose they are your cousins. For all I know, you may have fifty cousins by now."

"Fifty cousins? Wow!" breathed Manasseh, wide-eyed.

"Maybe," said Joseph. "Maybe one day we will find out."

Chapter 29

Hebrews in Egypt

Far away in the land of Canaan, the famine was finally forcing Jacob into action. The crops had failed and little fruit was to be found anywhere. Grass was sparse and in great demand. The family was running short of food.

On the previous day, Jacob had heard news that there were stocks of grain in Egypt and that even foreigners could buy it. While lying in bed, wakeful in the early hours, Jacob had decided what needed to be done. It would take his sons away and leave few who could do the work, but the famine meant that there was little work to do anyway. Ten of his eleven sons – not Benjamin, of course – must travel to Egypt and buy grain. Their children were so numerous that food didn't last very long, and they would soon reach a critical stage.

So now Jacob was sitting with his eleven sons, about to announce his plans. Reuben had just observed to Levi that the grain had nearly run out, but apart from that, everyone was just sitting and looking helplessly at each other. Jacob felt his exasperation rising.

"Why do you just sit and look at one another?" he asked irritably. "I have heard that there is grain for sale in Egypt. Why don't you go down and buy grain for us there, so that we can live and not die?"

It is only fair to admit that the same thought had occurred to several of the brothers, who had also heard the news, but they had held their tongues out of respect for their father. Now they were free to agree.

"Yes," said Judah, who once again spent most of his time with the family following the death of his wife. "That would be the best thing to do. We should all go to Egypt while you stay here with the women and children."

"I wonder what the price of grain is in Egypt?" asked Simeon. "Any grain we can get around here is prohibitively expensive."

"And there's hardly any of it anyway," agreed Levi.

"Should we take any of our children with us?" queried Asher. "It would be good for them to see some more of the world. We don't travel much."

"No, I don't think so," answered Naphtali. "They might be needed here, and it'll be better if it's only us in case we need to do any negotiating."

"But Benjamin is not going with you," said Jacob firmly. "You know that I'm always afraid harm will come to him. He will stay here with me."

The ten brothers looked at each other and rolled their eyes. Though Jacob's constant molly-coddling of Benjamin might be understandable in some ways, it certainly got on their nerves.

"It suits me not to go now, father," said Benjamin. "Another baby is due very soon."

"Does anyone know where we have to go?" asked Naphtali.

"No idea," replied Issachar. "We'll just have to see what happens."

Dan added, "I hear that Egypt has collected huge amounts of grain during the last few years. It's almost as if they knew the famine was coming."

"Yes, it's uncanny," agreed his brother Naphtali. "They say there's one man who organised it all. He's the governor of the land, I believe."

"But how could he have known?" asked Reuben, "It's not as if they would have been warned by El Shaddai, so how could their foolish gods know anything like that?"

"Apparently they have some pretty clever magicians there," said Zebulun.

"It takes more than just a magician to know the future," said Jacob. "And that's what we don't know, so you'll have to go and get the grain. Hopefully the famine will break before next year anyway."

CR

Thus it was that Joseph's brothers made the journey to Egypt as he had made it more than two decades before. But though they made the journey with some uncertainty, they suffered none of the fear and pain that had plagued Joseph because of their betrayal.

On the way, they met other travellers bent on the same mission. Canaan was in the grip of famine, and everyone had heard that there was grain in the land of Egypt. When they came to the border, they were told that all foreigners wishing to buy grain had to go to the central storehouses and seek permission from the governor of the land, the one they had heard about in Canaan. The border guards reassured them that nobody was ever refused, but that the governor wanted to make sure there was no skulduggery going on – no spying or deceptive trading.

Almost a month had been spent on the road by the time they stood before the governor and then bowed down before him with their faces to the ground. The governor was clean shaven and dressed in rich linen. He welcomed them with ceremony, speaking to them through an interpreter, but there was a doubtful look in his eye and his voice was harsh. With growing concern, the brothers wondered what was wrong. Had they not been assured that the governor never refused to sell grain to foreigners? Yet he was peppering them with suspicious questions as they stood quietly before him.

"Where do you come from?" he asked, and the translator conveyed both the words and the harshness of his tone.

Reuben replied defensively, "From the land of Canaan, to buy food."

For Joseph, the harsh voice was an attempt to cover up his real voice and the raw emotion that filled him at the sudden appearance of his brothers. This was the opportunity he had been waiting for ever since it had first occurred to him that he might receive a visit from his family if the famine was to spread over a wider area than just the land of Egypt.

"You are spies," he snarled, and the interpreter snarled likewise.

"No," the ten replied in horror. The interpreter captured their horror perfectly as he translated the word.

"You have come to spy out the weaknesses in our land." The voice was fiercely accusatory, and the interpreter excelled himself in accusation.

"No, my lord," denied the brothers, drawing in their breaths. "We, your servants, have come to buy food, nothing more." The voices were ingratiating and the translator got it nicely.

"We are all sons of one man," said Simeon.

"We are honest men," continued Judah. A bit of a stretch this one, but the translator told it without blinking.

"Your servants have never been spies." Enunciated with some injured pride and some genuine surprise, this sentence really tested the translator's mettle, but he made it through tolerably.

Joseph responded stubbornly, "No, you have come to see where the land is undefended." Stubbornness oozed out of every syllable of the translator's idiomatic Hebrew.

The brothers tried again, really worried by this time.

"We, your servants, are twelve brothers, the sons of one man in the land of Canaan," said Reuben, trying to speak slowly and calmly and doing his best to sound convincing, despite the quavering of his voice. "Our youngest brother is with our father, and one is no more." He inclined his head in pious acknowledgement of death and the translator did the same.

"No!" said Joseph categorically. "It is as I said to you: you are spies. However, we will test you by this: by the life of Pharaoh, you shall not go from this place unless your youngest brother comes here. Send one of you and let him bring your brother, while you remain locked up here, that your words may be tested, whether there is truth in you or not. Otherwise, by the life of Pharaoh, surely you are spies." Categoric was bread and butter to the translator, and the brothers had no difficulty understanding that the governor had pronounced judgement.

At Joseph's command, guards took the ten brothers and locked them all in a cell together for three days. Compared with the time spent by Joseph as a slave or in The Pit, it was nothing in either length of incarceration or depth of uncertainty; it was just a teaser. But it was a salutary lesson for the brothers. They had no idea what was going to happen. As far as they were concerned, Joseph had said that something was going to happen and then locked them up without letting them do what he suggested. Had there been a problem with translation, or had he changed his mind? There were arguments and opinions aplenty that first night. Ten in a cell was crowded, and the facilities in the cell were no better – but no worse either – than Joseph had endured for years.

Joseph visited the prison each day, but made sure that the news never reached the prisoners. How were they behaving? How was their health? What were they saying?

On the third day Joseph sent his steward to call them into his presence again, and the translator listened carefully as Joseph proclaimed his decision to the brothers. "Do this and you will live, for I fear God: if you are honest men, let one of your brothers remain confined where you are in custody, and let the rest go and carry grain for the famine of your households, and bring your youngest brother to me. So your words will be verified, and you shall not die."

After his words had been translated, Joseph gave them some time to discuss the proposal amongst themselves, allowing them to believe they could speak with freedom because they would not be understood. Shamelessly he listened to their discussion, eager to hear how they would decide what to do and interested to see whether they would suggest who should be the unlucky one to remain behind.

But he was utterly amazed by what he heard, as they said to one another, "We are truly guilty concerning our brother. We saw his distress, when he begged us to free him, and we did not listen. That is why this distress has come upon us."

More than twenty years after their betrayal of him, one unpleasant event had been enough to waken their feelings of guilt so that each of them saw a connection between their past treatment of him and their present trouble. Maybe he had not been the only one who had suffered greatly over the years!

Then Reuben answered the rest, "Did I not tell you not to sin against the boy? But you did not listen. So now there comes a reckoning for his blood."

So Reuben *had* stood up for him! Joseph still didn't know what had gone wrong with Reuben's plans to free him, but it was good to know that his oldest brother had recommended against the barbarism they had practised. Then suddenly, it was all too much. Joseph turned away and began to weep, hurrying to leave the room.

Once he had recovered, he returned to them. They agreed to his terms – not that they had much choice – so he took Simeon from them and bound him before their eyes. Reuben had won freedom for himself through his mercy, unsuccessful though it had been. Simeon was the next oldest and should have known better. Joseph also remembered Simeon's part in the annihilation of the men of Shechem and thought that it would do him good to suffer this treatment for a while. Once Simeon had been taken away in chains, it was a thoroughly subdued group of brothers who stood before Joseph, waiting to be allowed to leave.

"We will sell you one large bag of grain each; this is the limit we are enforcing at the moment," said Joseph. It was a limit he wanted to put on his brothers in particular, because he wanted them to return quickly and he was suspicious that only necessity would achieve that. "Each of you must give his money to my steward." Once more, Joseph went over the agreement on which they were being freed, then he left the room to arrange for the grain they were to buy.

Finding Setut, his steward, Joseph gave orders to fill their bags with grain, to replace every man's money in his sack, and to give them all provisions for the journey. It was done and the brothers took the sacks of grain they were given. After loading their donkeys with the grain, they departed thankfully.

Joseph watched them go and wondered when he would see them next. Would they come back or would fear keep them away? And what would they do about the money he had returned? There are many ways to test a man, and Joseph was trying several, eager to see whether his brothers had learned any lessons since they had so cruelly sold him into slavery. He was hoping to get good results.

The nine remaining brothers set off for Canaan, a little chastened and in a hurry to get back home. Despite the vital sacks of grain they had procured, there was no joy evident – in fact the entire party was rather quiet.

That night, they stopped at a lodging place and unloaded the donkeys. Shortly afterwards, Reuben went to care for his donkey. He opened his sack to give the animal some grain, but as he did so, he saw the gleam of silver mixed in with it. Quickly he picked out all the coins he could find and counted them. There were exactly the number he had given to the governor's steward earlier that day.

Immediately he ran to his brothers and said to them, "My money has been put back; here it is in the mouth of my sack!"

"It can't be," said Judah, and ran to his sack. Pulling it open, he quickly searched for silver coins, but saw none. "None here," he said. Each of the others likewise ran and opened his sack, but none of them found any silver in the neck of his sack. Many heads were shaken as they looked at each other and wondered.

"What is this that God has done to us?" said Levi, trembling, terrified that soon the governor's men would arrive, this time calling them thieves as well as spies.

Night passed without interruption, and early the next morning, the brothers quickly packed up and left. Four weeks later they came to their father Jacob and told him all that had happened to them.

They repeated the governor's accusation that they were spies and his demand that Benjamin be brought if ever they wanted any more grain – or to get Simeon back. They also told of the money found in the neck of Reuben's sack.

Later, as all of the other brothers emptied their sacks, lo and behold, every man found a bundle of money buried deep in his sack. And when they and their father saw the bundles of money, they were afraid.

"You have bereaved me of my children," Jacob said. "Joseph is no more, and Simeon is no more, and now you are trying to take Benjamin away. Everything is going wrong."

Reuben made an offer that was generous, but not very helpful: "You can kill my two sons if I don't bring Benjamin back to you. Put him in my hands, and I will bring him back to you."

In his mind, Jacob dismissed the offer. What advantage was there in killing two grandsons as well if he lost a son? "My son shall not go down with you, for his brother is dead, and he is the only one left. If harm should happen to him on the journey that you are to make, you would bring down my grey hairs to the grave with sorrow."

Chapter 30

Back to Egypt

The sacks of grain were big, but there were so many mouths to feed that the extra food was gone within three months.

"It's time for you to go back and get some more grain," said Jacob to Judah one day. "Go and buy us a little food. Surely the famine must end soon?"

"Only if you will let Benjamin go too – there is no point, otherwise," said Judah. "The man spelled it out to us very clearly. If we return without Benjamin, we won't get any food at all. All foreigners have to go to the governor to get permission to buy grain, and the governor told us that he won't even see us unless our brother is with us."

"Oh, why did you ever tell him that you had a brother?" asked Jacob, peevishly. Of course, he already knew the answer, but Judah told him again anyway.

"We didn't go out of our way to tell him, but he was asking us questions about our family, our father, other brothers, and so on. We just answered his questions. How could we know that he would make such a big thing of it?" Judah sighed, and continued, "Look, father, send the boy[12] with me, and we will leave immediately so that we

---

[12] Benjamin would have been at least 25 years old by this time, but older

may live and not die. I will be a pledge of his safety. From my hand you shall require him. If I do not bring him back to you and set him before you, then let me bear the blame forever. I know that won't help much, but if we had not delayed, we would now have returned twice." This was a bit of an exaggeration, but it made the point.

Jacob argued and complained, but Judah was implacable, and in the end Jacob had to give in. "If it must be so," he said, "then do this: take some of the best fruits of the land in your bags, and carry a present down to the man: a little balm and a little honey, gum, myrrh, pistachio nuts, and almonds. With this famine it will be little enough, but it is the best we can do."

"And what about the money, father?"

"Take double the money with you – the money that was returned as well. Perhaps it was an oversight. Take Benjamin too, and go back to the man." Jacob shook his head and looked a broken man. "May El Shaddai grant you mercy before the man, and may he let you leave with both Simeon and Benjamin. And as for me, if I am bereaved of my children, I am bereaved."

The brothers wasted no time obeying, in case Jacob should change his mind. They took twice the money, as well as Benjamin their youngest brother, and hurried off towards Egypt.

Joseph was waiting for them. He had been counting the days since they had left, hoping against hope that they would come back before the food ran out. Nevertheless, he was not surprised when that possibility faded. But Joseph had patience. He had waited 22 years to see his brother Benjamin – he could wait another month or two. Oh, the yearning, though! His only true brother, the only other son of his mother. He had been just a toddler when

---

brothers never forget that younger brothers are younger.

Joseph had been sold into Egypt, but now he would be a grown man. Would he be married? Might he even have children? Would he be tall or short? Thin or fat? Joseph's mind raced with all the things he had not been able to ask his brothers, yet longed to know.

Then one day, they finally arrived. Joseph got the message mid-morning and went to see them at once. As he entered the room, he saw Benjamin and could not take his eyes off him. This was his little brother, the one he had bounced on his knee and led around by the hand; the one who reminded him of his mother in appearance and the occasional gesture. He stared fixedly at Benjamin for several seconds before his emotions rose within him and he knew he had to leave. The brothers looked at each other in bewilderment as, without word or sign, he turned on his heel and swept out of the room again, looking steadfastly away from them.

Taking a deep breath, he went to Setut, his steward, and began to issue orders. "Kill the fattened calf and make it ready for us to eat. I will eat with them at noon. And bring the men to my house – I won't see them in the governor's offices anymore."

Setut rushed around making preparations while Joseph tried to compose himself.

෨

"It's all part of a plot, I reckon," muttered Gad, apprehensively.

They were walking away from the governor's offices with Setut and a translator. Setut had delivered Joseph's message that they were to meet him at his house. Joseph's strange behaviour had already made them wonder, and this even stranger demand had rung alarm bells in their minds.

"I think you're right," agreed Dan, quietly, making sure that the translator, walking in front of them, could not hear him. "It must be because of the money that was replaced in our sacks last time we came."

"Maybe once he gets us into his house his men will attack us, make us slaves and take our donkeys," suggested Zebulun.

"What should we do?" asked Gad.

"Let's start by telling them that we found the money in our sacks," proposed Levi.

"Yes," said Naphtali. "And then we can show them that we've brought back the money."

"It might make them believe that we're genuine," observed Reuben.

Judah tied it all together: "That sounds good. I'll talk to the steward as soon as we get to the governor's house."

A short time later, they arrived at Joseph's house. The steward led them to the gate and then said through the interpreter, "Just wait here for a moment, please." He turned to walk away, but Judah spoke up.

"Oh, excuse me please, sir," he said, and the steward turned back again. "We came to Egypt the first time to buy food, and when we were returning, we got to the lodging place and opened our sacks, and we found each man's money in the mouth of his sack – our money in full weight!" Judah let some of their amazement show in his voice. He continued confidingly, "So we have brought the money back again with us, along with other money for buying more food."

"We do not know who put our money in our sacks," added Reuben, worriedly.

Once the interpreter had finished conveying these messages, Setut smiled and replied, "Peace to you, do not be afraid. Your God and the God of your father must have put treasure in your sacks for you. I received your money." It was true, he thought, as he turned again and walked away: he had received the money alright, he had just made sure it was put in their sacks afterward as his master had ordered. Truth was important to the master, as everyone knew, and over the years during which Setut had worked for Joseph he had gradually found that it had begun to matter more to him too. He knitted his brows as he walked to the prison, mulling over all the changes that had happened in Egypt and in his own life because of this one strange foreigner. As he waited at the prison for Simeon to clean off his prison dirt, he wondered what his master was up to. It was all rather puzzling. These men obviously meant something to Joseph, but what?

Simeon was very glad to see the steward – an Egyptian jail was not the most pleasant place to spend a few months! He had even begun to wonder if he had been forgotten or whether something had gone wrong with his brothers. Much of the time he had spent feeling sorry for himself, but sometimes he had wondered what had happened to Joseph when he and his brothers had sent him to this place as a slave. Had Joseph spent time in an Egyptian jail? Probably not – most likely the boy had immediately been sold to work on the massive buildings these Egyptians seemed to spend all their time constructing. He imagined that a slave's life expectancy would be limited with such strenuous work, baking in the sun every day and working with enormous blocks of stone that could snuff out your life in a moment if you made a wrong move. The more he pondered, the more certain he was that Joseph must be dead, and he felt more guilt than ever before. Finally, he had admitted his crime, and found that he was sorry. If only he could do something to fix things up – but by this time Joseph must be dead, far beyond the reach of any help.

All in all, it was a much more humble Simeon that Setut led back to his master's house and presented to the waiting brothers, wearing the Egyptian clothing Setut had provided for him. They were glad to see him, but there was still a subdued feeling in the air. The steward's reassurances had not completely calmed their fears, and they were unsure of what would happen next.

Opening the gate, Setut led them and their donkeys inside the compound of Joseph's house. The donkeys were taken away to the stables, there to be made comfortable and given fodder.

"Come inside and get ready for Zaphenath-paneah's arrival. He will return at noon and is to eat here. You are honoured indeed. You too will eat here – oh, and you don't need to worry about any food customs, we will take care of all that for you."

The interpreter gave them the news in Hebrew and obediently they entered the palatial house – so different from their own rustic tents in Canaan – where they were given water to drink and more for washing their feet. The comfort was a little overwhelming, but they couldn't relax yet. First, they presented their money to Joseph's steward, who accepted the money they had brought for new grain but refused the money they had found in their sacks and brought back.

Next, they must go to the stables to unpack Jacob's present for the governor and arrange it attractively, to win the man's favour as much as possible. Asher would be the best man for that, the brothers agreed – he had a feel for such things that none of the others could equal.

Feeling a little more relaxed after washing their dusty feet, they went out to the stables and gathered the gifts their father had sent. Despite the seriousness of the famine, they felt that the size of the present was quite impressive. Joseph's servants provided them with several tables in a side room of the stables, and they all trooped into the room carrying the many parcels. To tell the truth, they felt rather more comfortable in the stables than in the opulent magnificence of that massive house.

Asher gave them instructions where each parcel should be put, and unpacked them all with care. The honey was sealed in elegant clay pots and the pistachio nuts were arranged in small decorated baskets along with the almonds. On another table, the containers of myrrh reposed. They had been sealed as well as Jacob's servants knew how, but still the fragrance escaped to fill the air. Balm from Gilead and gum were arrayed nearby, and the final presentation was both impressive and attractive. Asher continued to hover around the tables, nervously adjusting the placement of a pot here, a basket there, until finally his brothers told him to sit down and forget about it. The arrangement of the present was, they said, delightful. Asher obeyed, but he continued to look critically across at his handiwork, and couldn't resist popping up for further minor adjustments from time to time as they waited apprehensively for noon and the governor to arrive.

☙

A little before noon, Joseph arrived and went to his rooms.

On being advised of his arrival, the brothers carefully carried the elaborately arranged tables into the house and through to the exquisite banqueting hall with its superbly plastered and painted walls and the high roof that gave it such a feeling of spaciousness. Asher fussed over the placement of the tables for as long as he dared, before finally leaving them to stand with the rest of his brothers, waiting for Joseph to enter.

A single trumpet blast announced his coming, and the brothers were reminded again of the power of this man.

All Egypt fell at his feet and praised his name. If he desired it, a man lost his head; if he desired it, a man was covered with riches. This man was Egypt; Pharaoh was king in name only. The leadership and direction came from this governor – Zaphenath-paneah, saviour, creator, revealer. No-one so much as moved in Egypt without his permission.

Zaphenath-paneah entered quite casually, in no way requiring the ostentatious obeisance that normally greeted a man of his rank. But his brothers fell on their knees and bowed down to the ground before him, not one of them thinking even for an instant of that long-ago day when their brother Joseph had told them about a dream where their sheaves had bowed down to his sheaf. Yet in their eagerness to show respect to the great man who was giving them an audience, they fulfilled the very words at which they had scoffed.

If their kneeling struck any chord in his memory, Joseph gave no indication of it, but was merely an interested, welcoming host. "Welcome to Egypt. Are you all well?"

A polite chorus of yeses came in response.

"And is your father well, the old man you spoke of? Is he still alive?" The concern in his voice surprised them, but they had heard rumours of this man's kindness – reports that seemed so much at odds with his treatment of them and his accusations of spying.

"Yes," said Reuben, finally, "our father is well and still very much alive."

Joseph smiled and the brothers bowed to him again, even more deeply this time, prostrating themselves before him on the decorated flooring.

And then Joseph did what he had wanted to do for so long. He walked to Benjamin and took him by the hand, lifting him from his prostrate position on the floor. It was hard for him to believe that this fine young man had been the baby and toddler with whom he had spent so much time, playing with and loving him. "Is this your youngest brother?" he asked the others. "The one you spoke to me about?" Some heads nodded and Joseph said to Benjamin, "God be gracious to you, my son!"

Then suddenly, once again, it was all too much, and Joseph hurried out. Unable to control the warmth of his feeling for his long-lost brother, he rushed to his bedchamber to weep.

His brothers looked at each other in bemusement as Joseph left, almost in the middle of his sentence. The governor was behaving very strangely today. Was there anything sinister about it or had he just had a bad night? Possibly he was sick and it was a need to vomit that took him away. For the first time in the whole saga, a few of the brothers began to think of someone other than themselves and to wonder about the health of this great governor.

It took Joseph some time to control his emotions, and then he washed his face and returned to the banqueting hall. There, he found that some of the moveable screens which normally lined the walls of the hall had already been arranged to form three separate eating areas, so that no-one in any of the areas would be able to see anyone in the other areas.

"Serve the food," he ordered the servants standing near the door that led to the massive kitchens beyond. Many important people came to visit the governor, and many of them were invited to the less formal meals that were served in Joseph's own house. Food was a serious matter to the Egyptians, as were the customs for eating. Egyptians feel very strongly about who they should eat with, and refuse to eat with a Hebrew, however important. Thus, although Joseph was second in command to Pharaoh and governor over the whole land, still no Egyptian would eat with him, not even a slave or a criminal. Joseph was used to this, but it caused trouble at times when high-ranking foreigners must be entertained while still maintaining the niceties of Egyptian food culture. So it was that, as the food was served, Joseph's brothers were led to one area, while Joseph's Egyptian deputies and servants moved into another, and Joseph himself was served in a third area.

As the brothers were led one by one to their seats, they gradually began to realise that they were witnessing another astonishing feature of this strange day. Reuben was led to a seat first and fussed over by Joseph's servant, who made sure that he was comfortable and familiar with all of the eating implements favoured by the Egyptians. Next, Simeon was taken to his seat, and then, one by one, each of the brothers was seated in the order of his birth until finally, Benjamin received the same gracious treatment and the group of eleven brothers was complete.

The brothers looked at each other as they slowly recognised the significance of what had happened. Yes, Benjamin was the youngest – and Joseph had known that because they had told him so – but the other ten brothers had all been born within six years to three different mothers. Yet Joseph's servant had seated them in the exact order of their age! Their eyes widened as they realised the impossibility of this astonishing feat. How could he have done it? Maybe it was true what the Egyptians said about him, that Joseph knew what people were thinking and even what they said in their own bedchamber.

Joseph's Egyptian visitors were served their food directly, but the rest of the food was delivered to Joseph's massive table. The food was piled up on plates or in steaming pots, a multitude of delicious smells blending into an irresistible aroma that spread throughout the huge hall.

Large portions were served from Joseph's table to his brothers – strictly in age order. But when it was Benjamin's turn to be served, the servant continued to serve, spoon, ladle, scoop, supply and deliver portion after portion. Once he finished, it was clear to everyone that his serve was five times as large as anybody else's. Yet another item to be added to the list of peculiarities of this most peculiar of days.

Drinks were not lacking either, and Joseph drank with his guests from a large silver cup that seemed to have pride of place on his table. The cup was richly ornamented and the Egyptian servants who filled it from time to time treated it with great respect.

Benjamin watched this performance several times, intrigued that a cup should be treated with such honour. Joseph, who was keeping an eye on Benjamin much of the time, noticed his interest and called him up to the table, showing him the cup and allowing him to feel its weight. It was clearly a special and valuable object.

Everyone ate and drank happily with Joseph. For Joseph himself, though, this was just another successful step in his plan.

Through the afternoon and on into the evening the feast continued. From time to time, the guests left their screened areas to join together in the open area of the hall, where entertainment was provided by dancers and singers. The banquet was grand beyond anything the tent-dwelling brothers had ever experienced or even imagined.

During the afternoon, Joseph called Setut and spoke to him quietly, clearly laying out his instructions. The brothers' sacks were to be filled with grain, as much as it would be possible for their donkeys to carry. The money each had paid was then to be placed in the neck of his sack and – here Joseph lowered his voice even further – Joseph's silver cup was to be placed in the sack of Benjamin, the youngest brother, along with his money.

Setut did all that Joseph had told him to do.

That night, once the banquet was over, the brothers slept in Joseph's house, having been told that their grain had been packed and that they would be leaving early in the morning.

Chapter 31

The trap

As soon as it was light, the brothers got up and prepared to leave, finding that their donkeys had already been loaded with grain.

Setut bade them goodbye, and Joseph himself watched from a window as they led their donkeys out of the gate of his compound. Little did they know that they would soon be back again. Joseph smiled to himself and prayed that his plans would be successful.

Timing was important for the story to be credible, so Joseph waited until he knew they would have left the city and travelled a short distance along the road before calling Setut and giving him more instructions. The man listened with an expressionless face and left immediately, taking with him the interpreter who spoke Hebrew so well. As he did so, he thought to himself that Joseph was a good master, but sometimes did things that were quite incomprehensible.

His chariot rushed through the streets of the city, hurtled out of the gate and hurried along the road. It was not long before he saw the men in the distance, and he soon caught up with them.

"Hey, Hebrews!" he called. He knew enough Hebrew for that. "Stop!"

The brothers stopped and turned, worry showing clearly on each face. "What do you want?" asked Judah.

"Why have you repaid evil for good?" the steward asked. He found that speaking through an interpreter slowed communication enough to make it easier to carefully follow all of Joseph's instructions. "Is my master's silver cup not the one from which my lord drinks, and by which he practises divination? You have done evil in this."

"Why do you speak such words as these, my lord?" asked Judah. "We would never do such a thing!"

"Remember," interrupted Reuben, "we even brought back the money that we had found in our sacks. We brought it back to you all the way from the land of Canaan. So why would we steal silver or gold from your lord's house? If any of your servants is found with the cup he shall die, and the rest of us will be my lord's servants."

Setut blandly agreed, but then completely changed the conditions. "Let it be as you say: he who is found with it shall be my servant, and the rest of you shall be innocent."

It wasn't worth arguing, and actions were better than words if they wanted to clear their names, so each of the brothers quickly lowered his sack to the ground and opened it.

Setut began his search with Reuben's sack, as Joseph had instructed. The glint of silver was clear in the neck of the sack, but Setut felt around it, looking only for the cup. Reuben was watching closely, and his eyes widened as he saw the silver coins. Why was Joseph's steward ignoring them? The search was soon over, and no sign of a silver cup had been found.

Simeon's sack was next, and it was clear that Simeon had already found the silver coins it contained: his eyes were wide and a look of doom had spread across his face.

Possibly he was remembering the months spent in that horrible Egyptian jail and wondering if he was about to spend more time there. But Setut pushed the coins roughly aside and searched through the grain instead, reaching deep into the sack as the seed flowed like water around his arm. Once he had finished, he also ran his hands over the outside of the sack to see whether any hard object was inside, but there was nothing.

So it went on. In every sack, the coins were ignored and the remainder of the sack was searched for Joseph's silver cup. Each man watched in turn as his sack was searched. Although it didn't seem important at the time, the brothers did notice that once again they had been placed in order of birth. Was this evidence of the divination Joseph's steward had referred to?

Finally there was only one sack left. One more search to be made before they could go on their way, exonerated. So why did they all feel so nervous? The steward held the neck of Benjamin's sack wide open. The now-familiar coins were pushed aside as he reached down into the sack. His searching fingers pushed aside the grain and the watching brothers saw his expression suddenly change. His lips were pursed and his eyes fixed firmly on Benjamin's as he slowly withdrew his hand. As the grain bulged and then parted to reveal a silver cup, there was a sharp intake of breath from each of the brothers. Setut held up the cup and looked accusingly at Benjamin.

"I think we will need to go back to Zaphenath-paneah," he said grimly.

There were loud cries from several mouths as the brothers recognised their doom, then one after another, they revealed their inexpressible sorrow by tearing their clothes.

No-one had a word to say. It wasn't worth it. They had not filled the sacks themselves and there was no way that Benjamin could ever have had access to the governor's cup – but that would be no excuse. Bitterly, the brothers began to realise that it must be a plot, as they had suggested earlier – before they had been lulled into a false sense of security by the generous feast they had enjoyed. Now they were trapped, and nothing that they could say would save them. Silently they loaded the donkeys again and returned to the city, each brother keeping his thoughts to himself and Setut doing the same. The steward actually felt a little sorry for the men, but if Joseph was orchestrating this setup, then he must have a good reason for it, and his steward wasn't going to do anything to interfere.

❧

Joseph was still at home when they arrived. Setut led the brothers into a large room where several guards were waiting, and the translator followed. Setut spoke quietly to the guards and they took up positions by the doors, leaving the eleven brothers standing huddled in the middle of the room.

Judah stood and thought. Life had become a nightmare and he could see no possible way out. Ever since his brutal heartlessness with Joseph so many years before, everything had gone wrong. He thought back with disgust on his suggestion that there was no profit in killing Joseph and that instead they should make some money by selling him. He was bitterly ashamed now of the proposal to sell him as a slave, but even more upset by the idea behind it: that if they sold him, they would make money out of him while knowing that he would probably die shortly afterwards anyway. The thought had preyed on his mind and plagued him for years. He had tried to turn over a new leaf and had believed that he had succeeded, but then there had been the incident where he had casually ordered Tamar's death, though she had been righteous and he evil. Once again, the guilt had tortured him, and in his repentance he had thought such failures were behind him. He had been seeking a higher responsibility and a greater care for others when he had offered to look after Benjamin on this trip. And now he had failed in this also. Maybe the only answer was to try to take all of the blame or responsibility on himself. Benjamin could not be left to rot in an Egyptian dungeon. Despite some of the things which had happened, he had the feeling that this governor really was a kind and gentle man. Maybe the governor would be willing to give up his claim to Benjamin as long as someone was punished, and maybe he, Judah, could be that someone. It would be the first really positive thing he had ever done in his life – Joseph had always been the one who had done those sorts of things. Perhaps he would get on better with Joseph now – if only he hadn't sentenced him to death as a slave. He shook his head and continued to dwell on his regrets.

Judah wasn't the only brother whose mind was filled with thoughts of Joseph and the guilt they had all incurred through their treatment of him, though he was the only one in whom it led to action. The picture of Joseph, helpless at the bottom of that cruel hole, begging for his life while they laughed and jeered, was in the minds of several, for guilt is a terrible burden to bear.

Finally, Joseph entered, surrounded by his servants and deputies. Judah led the way by falling to the ground in front of him, and all the other brothers did the same.

"What is this that you have done?" Joseph asked. "Do you not know that a man like me can indeed practise divination?"

Judah was determined to do what he could and replied first, still on his knees: "What shall we say to my lord, or how can we clear ourselves? God has found out the guilt of your servants; behold, we are my lord's servants, both we and he also in whose hand the cup has been found." It was a chance that he had to take. Whatever happened, he must get around Reuben's rash statement that the one who had the cup should die. That was of utmost importance, even if it left them all as slaves.

"Oh, no!" said Joseph. "How could I ever do that? Only the man in whose sack the cup was found shall be my servant. But as for the rest of you, go up in peace to your father."

Then Judah rose and approached Joseph. The guards hurried towards him, but Joseph waved them away.

With a humility that had never before been heard from his mouth, Judah said, "Oh, my lord, please let your servant speak a word in my lord's ears, and let not your anger burn against your servant. My lord asked his servants, saying, 'Have you a father, or a brother?' And we said to my lord, 'We have a father, an old man, and a young brother, the child of his old age. His brother is dead, and he alone is left of his mother's children, and his father loves him.' Then you said to your servants, 'Bring him down to me, that I may see him.' We said to my lord, 'The boy cannot leave his father or his father would die.' Then you said to your servants, 'Unless your youngest brother comes down with you, you shall not see my face again.' "

"Yes," agreed Joseph. "That is what I said."

"When we went back to your servant my father, we told him what you said. And when our father said, 'Go again, buy us a little food,' we said, 'We cannot go down. We will only go down if our youngest brother goes with us. For we cannot see the man's face unless our youngest brother is with us.' Then your servant my father said to us, 'You know that my wife bore me two sons. One left me, and I said, "Surely he has been torn to pieces," and I have never seen him since. If you take this one also from me, and harm happens to him, you will bring down my grey hairs in evil to Sheol.'

"So as soon as I come to your servant my father, and the boy is not with us, then, as his life is bound up in the boy's life, as soon as he sees that the boy is not with us, he will die, and your servants will bring down the grey hairs of your servant our father with sorrow to Sheol. For your servant became a pledge of safety for the boy to my father, saying, 'If I do not bring him back to you, then I shall bear the blame before my father all my life.' Now therefore, please let your servant remain instead of the boy as a servant to my lord, and let the boy go back with his brothers. For how can I go back to my father if the boy is not with me? I fear to see the disaster that would come to my father." Judah took a deep breath and prayed that his words would convince the man. For once he felt that what he had done was right. It was a much better feeling than the guilt that had plagued him so often.

Looking at Judah, Joseph remembered the words his brother had spoken so long before, offering him, Joseph, as a slave. But now he was offering to become a slave himself to save his father – the very father he had so callously caused to suffer when disposing of Joseph. The change in his brother tugged at his heartstrings and he could no longer control himself.

"Everybody go out and leave us alone," he cried, his voice breaking.

Joseph sobbed as his deputies reluctantly left the room with the servants and guards. The Egyptians could not understand what was happening. Joseph had never behaved so strangely before. What could it be? Quickly a message was sent to Pharaoh's household to inform him that Joseph was behaving very strangely – he seemed to be suffering from some sort of extreme grief or upset. Eleven Hebrews were having an audience with him.

Someone in Pharaoh's palace had a very good memory and remembered that Joseph was actually a Hebrew himself. Everyone knew he was a foreigner, but most had forgotten which was the land of his birth.

"Maybe he knows these people," someone guessed.

"Oh, I don't think so," said the servant from Joseph's house who had brought the news. "None of them seemed to recognise him. Maybe it has just triggered some terrible memories for Zaphenath-paneah. Wasn't he actually a slave sometime before he became second in command?"

As all of these guesses and speculations whirled around the palace, Joseph revealed his true identity to his brothers.

"I am Joseph!" he said, still sobbing. "Is my father really still alive?"

But his brothers could not answer him – the enormity of his revelation was still sinking in. All they could do was to stare at him.

"Come near to me, please," he begged. They approached hesitantly and Joseph continued, "I am Joseph, your brother, whom you sold into Egypt."

"But that's not possible," Judah protested. "Joseph is dead."

"How do you think I knew the order of your birth? And now do not be angry with yourselves because you sold me here, for God sent me before you to preserve life. The famine has been in the land these two years, and there are still five years in which there will be neither ploughing nor harvest. So it was not you who sent me here, but God. He has made me a father to Pharaoh, and lord of all his house and ruler over all the land of Egypt." Joseph looked around at his brothers and saw that they were finally beginning to believe him. He realised that it must be hard to adjust one's ideas to admit that someone is alive when one has been sure for so many years that he is dead.

"Here is what you must do," continued Joseph. "Hurry and go to my father and say to him, 'Thus says your son Joseph, God has made me lord of all Egypt. Come down to me; don't delay. You shall live in the land of Goshen, and you shall be near me, you and your children and your children's children, and your flocks, your herds, and all that you have. There I will provide for you, for there are still five years of famine to come. Otherwise you and your household will come to poverty.' "

"Are you really my brother Joseph?" asked Benjamin. "I don't remember you at all, but Dad has told me lots of stories about you and our mother."

"Yes, I am Joseph," he answered, turning to look directly at his brother. "Joseph: slave, prisoner, governor. I have many more stories I could tell you now. But what about you? I want to hear what has happened to you since you were the cute little brother I knew and loved 22 years ago." He looked him up and down, seeing his height, the breadth of his shoulders, and the smile that often appeared and reminded Joseph of their mother.

"I suppose I grew up," laughed Benjamin, clearly convinced that this really was the brother he knew only from stories.

"We need to talk more, but for now we need to make some arrangements." Joseph turned back to the rest of his brothers and spoke to them all again. "You can all see, just as my brother Benjamin can see, that it is I, Joseph, speaking to you. You must tell my father of all my honour in Egypt, and of all that you have seen. Hurry and bring my father down here."

Then he went to Benjamin and hugged him and wept, while Benjamin wept too. After that, he kissed all of his brothers and wept over them as well. So many years had been missed, and so much hatred had taken so long to cure.

After that, his brothers talked with him.

Chapter 32

Egypt's joy

Setut the steward was the first one to think of an excuse to go in and check on Joseph. He knocked on the door, first quietly and then, when there was no response, more loudly.

All twelve brothers were busy talking, and Joseph's brothers had felt more joy in his company during that short period than they had done in all their lives before. Leaving the hatred behind had been the start of it, and gradually beginning to believe that he would not try to pay them back for their hatred had been the part that loosened their tongues. It was a belief that they would struggle to hold on to over the coming years as again and again the knowledge of the enormity of their sin overwhelmed their belief in forgiveness.

Eventually, though, Joseph noticed the banging on the door, crossed to it and opened it. "Yes?" he asked.

"Excuse me please, sir," asked Setut with a straight face. "Did you want lunch served for you and your visitors, or should we be putting them in prison instead?"

Joseph laughed and said, "Setut, these are my brothers. I can't put them in prison."

"Your brothers, sir? The ones who…" he stopped and looked embarrassed.

Joseph smiled and said, "We all do wrong from time to time, don't we, Setut? But yes, these men, my brothers, will eat lunch with me at noon."

"Then I had better go and let the cooks know about lunch, sir. And, sir, I'm sure that Pharaoh would like to hear your news. Can I make sure he is told?"

"Certainly," said Joseph, delighted. "He has been patient with me in my loneliness, so now he should hear of my happiness."

The kitchen heard first, because the food preparation couldn't wait, but Pharaoh himself and his household heard very shortly after that, and all were very pleased when they heard the report, "Joseph's brothers have come."

Immediately, Pharaoh sent a message to Joseph saying, "Don't let your brothers leave until you have seen me."

Later that afternoon, Joseph visited Pharaoh, who said to him, "Say to your brothers, 'Do this: load your donkeys and go back to the land of Canaan, and get your father and your households, and come to me, and I will give you the best of the land of Egypt, and you shall eat the fat of the land.' And you, Joseph, are commanded to say, 'Do this: take wagons from the land of Egypt for your little ones and for your wives, and bring your father, and come. Have no concern for your goods, for the best of all the land of Egypt is yours.' "

Pharaoh's generosity would make it take a little longer before the brothers could leave, but when they left, they would do so in style.

Chapter 33

Fetch Dad!

Judah had been thinking deeply since the discovery of the cup in Benjamin's sack. He had reviewed his life and his decisions many times and come to the conclusion that he had much to change in his life. He had also acknowledged that he had been jealous of Joseph for no other reason than that Joseph was a better person than he was – something that had taken quite a lot of courage to admit, even to himself. Joseph's reaction to the brothers who had injured him had also convinced him that Joseph would be a good man to copy as he tried to remodel his life.

Joseph had been in the perfect position to fully repay them for their cruelty to him, yet he had done nothing of the kind. True, he had tested them to see if they were still the same people they had been, and Judah wondered what he would have done if he had come to the conclusion that they were. What would have happened if Joseph had not heard of their feelings of guilt, of Reuben's failed attempt to free him, of Judah's willingness to be his slave to save Benjamin? He wasn't sure, but he was glad that they had at least begun to change.

However, Judah was determined that he was going to change more. He had had examples of righteousness before him throughout his life, but had ignored them when they didn't suit. Now he would pay attention to those examples and learn from them, starting with making friends with Joseph.

By the time they left Egypt, he was a fair way towards achieving that goal, although it wasn't always easy to get time with Joseph – as governor he was a very busy man. Even Benjamin found it hard to get much time with his special brother.

Joseph gave his brothers wagons, according to Pharaoh's command, and provisions for the journey as well. He also gave each of them a change of clothes, but to Benjamin he gave three hundred shekels of silver and five changes of clothes.

To his father, Joseph sent twenty donkeys loaded with the good things of Egypt, including grain, bread, and special provisions for the return journey. Then he sent his brothers away, accompanied by quite a few of his Egyptian servants because there were so many wagons and animals to care for.

As they departed, Joseph said to them, "Do not quarrel on the way."

◌℞

They returned to the land of Canaan and came to their father Jacob. When they arrived, it was instantly clear from the convoy of wagons and the Egyptian servants that something unexpected had happened.

He greeted them a little apprehensively, almost too bewildered to check that all his sons had returned safely; and then they told him, "Joseph is still alive, and he is ruler over all the land of Egypt." He listened, but he couldn't believe them. The torn and blood-stained coat had proved that Joseph was dead, though he had been reluctant to accept it – indeed, it had taken him years to really accept the fact – and now he could not go back. Joseph *must* be dead.

So they told him all the words of Joseph, and courageously but awkwardly explained the hatred, cruelty, lies and deception that had dispatched Joseph to Egypt in the first place and provided his father with the 'proof' of his death. Once again, it was Judah who revealed his improving character by giving the bulk of the explanation, holding back nothing of his own appalling part in it. Levi and Simeon gave a little support also, while the rest kept silent. The brothers had discussed endlessly on the way exactly how they should deliver the news to Jacob, and often the discussions had very nearly led to the quarrelling that Joseph had obviously been afraid of. As the only one with anything positive to present, Reuben had wanted to justify himself, but the other brothers had argued that, far from pleasing their father, it was likely to further reduce his opinion of his oldest son. Had Reuben not completely failed to stop the callous inhumanity that had condemned Joseph to life as a slave? Having an oldest son who cannot lead is like using a broken reed as a staff.

Jacob's incredulity and horror at their explanations were so deep that the brothers were worried for his well-being, but when he saw the wagons that Joseph had sent to carry him, his spirit revived. And Israel said, "It is enough; Joseph my son is still alive. I will go and see him before I die."

That was easy to say, but the task was not a small one – bigger by far than the dimly-remembered flight from Paddan-aram. Firstly there were the people: Jacob, his eleven sons with their wives and children, and many grandchildren as well, plus menservants and maidservants. In the end, there were several hundred people preparing to make the journey to Egypt, although no count of all the people was made in the end.

Tents, clothing, bedding, cooking equipment, farming goods, animals, and many, many other things were all packed. Finally, everything seemed to be ready and the long trip to Egypt began. Jacob looked soberly around the camp site that had now been stripped of all their goods. The land had been promised to Abraham, his grandfather, who had never owned any of it except the burial ground he had purchased in Hebron. Abraham and Sarah had both died in the land and been buried in that cave. Isaac and Rebecca had owned no more of the land either. Isaac had lived as a visitor in his own land all his life, living in tents and dying as a foreigner. All had been waiting for God to give them the land, while their relatives had gone elsewhere to take land for themselves. Why was it that the ones who were chosen by God were the only ones who were still waiting?

The convoy started and Jacob refused to look back as another chapter of his life closed: the next chapter would take him to Joseph, and he couldn't wait to see him!

಄

As they journeyed towards the south, they came to Beersheba, and Jacob offered sacrifices to God one last time before leaving the promised land. El Shaddai was the God both his father and his grandfather had worshipped, and Jacob was determined to follow in their footsteps to the end of his days.

While they were at Beersheba, God spoke to him, calling him "Israel", the name he had won from an angel by wrestling all night. Again, he had visions of the night and heard a voice which said, "Jacob, Jacob."

He replied, "Here I am."

"I am God," said the voice, "the God of your father. Do not be afraid to go down to Egypt, for there I will make you into a great nation. I myself will go down with you to Egypt, and I will also bring you up again, and Joseph's hand shall close your eyes."

Sometimes it was hard to understand exactly what God meant. He had spoken of bringing Jacob back to this land, but also that Joseph's hands would close Jacob's eyes for the last time in the sleep of death. Would they return before he died, with Joseph accompanying them, or was this the same promise that God had made to Abraham, that he would inherit the land only as part of resurrection and a new life?

Either way, the promise was one to look forward to.

The next morning, Jacob set out from Beersheba with his sons, their little ones, and their wives, in the wagons that Pharaoh had sent to carry him.

Chapter 34

Reunited

Egypt is quite a different land from Canaan. Whereas Canaan has hills and valleys, rivers and lakes, swamps and deserts, Egypt has only sand, flatness, and a river that breaks up into countless branches as it meanders its way sluggishly to the sea.

The areas around the Nile River are normally highly fertile, places where the annual floods constantly renew the soil and vegetation abounds. In this time of famine, however, the river was small and moved even more slowly than usual. There was no chance of farmers harvesting much water from the once mighty Nile to pour over the land, and no hope of the ordinary rapid growth of crops.

Judah was sent ahead to meet Joseph and find the way to the land of Goshen where they would live. When they arrived, Joseph travelled to Goshen to meet his father.

It is difficult to describe the reunion between a father and his beloved son after 22 years of separation. It is hard to begin to imagine the strength of the old man's emotion as his eyes finally behold the son he has longed to see for so long, but had been forced to give up hoping for. And it is equally hard to describe how a devoted son feels when he finally meets once more the father he has longed for through many years of separation and hard service.

As Jacob sat waiting on a wagon, he saw a uniformed troop of mounted soldiers approaching in strict formation. They swept off the road and moved to encircle the waiting wagons and people, slowing to a halt as they did so. The old man's fears were all reawakened, and for the moment he forgot the visitor he was expecting. Had something gone wrong with the arrangements? Were they to be apprehended and imprisoned?

An Egyptian, obviously important and dressed accordingly, came toward them in a chariot decorated with silver and gold. Others in slightly less magnificent clothes rode in chariots flanking the first but slightly behind.

The leading chariot came straight toward Jacob, first slowing to a walk and then stopping completely a few metres away. The exquisitely dressed man leaped down and strode eagerly towards him. His face was wreathed in smiles and looked vaguely familiar under the strange Egyptian headdress.

"Father!" said Joseph, and the old man suddenly understood.

"Joseph," he exclaimed, and held out his arms.

The elegant young nobleman ran the last few steps to his father and flung his arms around him. Jacob was glad he had been sitting down or he would have been knocked off his feet.

For a few moments there was silence as both were overcome with emotion. Then Jacob pulled away to get a proper look at his beloved son. "Is it really you, Joseph?"

"Yes, father, it is I. I have been made second in command in Egypt, so now I travel around with all of this entourage wherever I go. No longer can I travel by myself and do what I want."

"My son, I am so glad to see you, and so proud of what you have accomplished."

"Oh, my father, I have not achieved this, the God of Abraham, Isaac and Israel has done it."

" 'Israel' – you remember that name, do you?"

"Oh, yes. I think our descendants will probably be called the children of Israel when they return to Canaan. But in the meantime, we will live in Egypt under the care of El Shaddai. He sent me here before you all to preserve life. If I had not been sent here, we would all have died in Canaan because there would have been no grain in Egypt or anywhere in the world for us to buy. God did this, and God kept me safe through all the time in which I stayed here."

"What happened when you arrived here?"

"I was sold to a man called Potiphar, a commander of Pharaoh's guard. He was a kind master, and after a while he gave me more and more responsibility until I was in command of his entire house. That took several years." He paused, reluctant even now to tell the story of Zulaykha's actions.

"Don't stop, Joseph, keep going. I have missed so much of your life, and now I want to hear it all."

"A woman tried to seduce me – and no, I didn't give her any encouragement at all. She kept harassing and pestering me, but, with God's help, I kept saying 'No'."

"I'm glad of that, my son. Have you talked to Reuben or Judah about it?"

"No, I haven't – have they had similar experiences? In any case, they must choose their own way in life, though I have the feeling that Judah is trying to walk more in God's way now. I certainly hope so – it is such a rewarding way of life, even if it isn't always easy."

"Anyway, what happened next?"

"One day when all the men of the house were out, she tried to drag me into her room to do what she demanded.

Everything was going so badly that I had to just leave my coat and run. I ran out of that house as if I was being chased by a lion." Joseph smiled, but the smile held little real amusement.

"You did very well. Run away from temptation if it is ever becoming too great. I admire you for that, and your mother would too. I can almost hear her saying, 'Joseph, dear, I'm really proud of you.' " The old man's eyes misted over and he looked away into the distance, still missing his lost love.

"Well, it didn't get me out of trouble, I can tell you!" Joseph continued. "She made up a story that I had attacked her and that she had screamed until I ran away and left my coat behind. The next day I was put into a place they call 'The Pit', which is a dungeon where the king's prisoners are kept. I spent eight years there."

"Eight years on a false charge? Oh, my poor son." Jacob looked at Joseph with sympathy, understanding for the first time just how much Joseph had suffered though his brothers' cruelty, and the astonishing depth of his forgiveness. But he also saw that El Shaddai must have had a hand in it all. "It's amazing that you survived. In fact, I'm surprised they didn't execute you immediately on a charge like that."

"Well, maybe people didn't completely believe the charge. I really don't know. One way or another, though, I was kept in one of the deepest dungeons for quite a while, until gradually, I was allowed to move up a level or two — into cells that had some light."

"How long did that take?"

"About four years. And once that happened I was able to help the keeper of the prison from time to time. It gave me something to do, and after a while, I was more or less in charge of the prison, looking after any special prisoners personally and organising anything that needed organising. It's funny, but it seems that every time I stay in a place for a while, the leader of the place ends up using me as his personal assistant."

"More like his special gift from God, I'd say, given to solve all of his problems," Jacob retorted.

"You're exaggerating. But anyway, while I was in The Pit, there was a situation where I had to interpret two dreams. Do you remember the dreams I had when I was 17, Dad?"

"Yes, I remember alright – the one about your brothers' sheaves bowing down to your sheaves. They wouldn't ever do that, would they?"

"They have already, father. With all of the drama here when they were feeling worried, upset and guilty, they all bowed down to me more than once. It was such a humbling experience – which is peculiar. But to think that God has arranged everything, set it all up so long before, and then moved so many things in all our lives to achieve exactly what he wants! It is just astonishing. And using *me* too – that is what makes it so humbling. The God of Abraham using me. Abraham was God's friend and it is easy to understand why God would work with him, but me? It still gives me goose-bumps."

"I'm sorry, I seem to have distracted you from your story. What were you saying about dreams in The Pit?"

"There were two very special prisoners. One was Pharaoh's chief butler and the other was his chief baker. They had upset Pharaoh and so he had thrown them into prison to cool their heels. Back then Pharaoh was sometimes a little bit volatile. He's much more stable and consistent nowadays."

"You've changed Pharaoh too, have you?" Jacob smiled, only half teasing.

"Me? Of course not. But he certainly has changed, which is good, or I might have been thrown back in prison for making some wrong move at some time or other. Anyway, the butler and the baker had made wrong moves and were in prison with no release date set – much like me. The keeper of the prison had assigned them to me to look after, so I spent time with them and tried to keep them a little happier. One morning, they looked really upset, and each of them told me that he had had a worrying dream. The two dreams were different, but had some similar characteristics. I prayed and God gave me an understanding of their dreams, so I told them what would happen – and it did. After three days, the butler was given back his job in Pharaoh's court and the baker was hanged. It was Pharaoh's birthday, and he often does some specially kind things on his birthday. But he also gets rid of people he doesn't want, sometimes, so it doesn't pay to treat Pharaoh too casually."

"Were the butler and the baker happy that you had interpreted their dreams?"

"The butler was, of course, but the baker showed how much we deny things we don't like. When I first interpreted his dream he was worried, which showed that he believed what I had said. But then after a while he started to completely deny my interpretation, and pretty much said that I was a fool."

"I think I understand how he would have felt," said Jacob, shivering. "Knowing that you are going to die in three days would be frightening."

"You're right – I hope it never happens to me. Well, I did my best to calm him down and keep him busy, but I didn't have much success. He kept saying I was crazy, right up until the soldiers came to collect them both and take them to Pharaoh. They almost had to carry him. It was sad, but he really wasn't the sort of man that Pharaoh would want in his court. I know that now since I know Pharaoh so much better. And I don't think he was a very good worker either, and Pharaoh hates laziness."

"Well, he'll never see that with you, so no need to worry about that."

"Father, you don't need to praise me all the time," laughed Joseph. "I have many faults too, you know."

"Oh, I'm sure you have, but you really manage to hide them very well. What happened after that? Did the butler tell Pharaoh what had happened?"

"I asked him to," said Joseph, "but he didn't do so. As far as I can tell, he just forgot about me. Now that's a good thing to think about when one wants to learn humility."

"Yes, God will always give us things to remind us of our limitations. I don't know how many times he has done so with me. My brother planning to kill me; Laban cheating me with Leah and then changing my wages ten times; my sons telling me that you had been eaten by a wild animal. So many things to remind me that I am not perfect and that happiness is not what life is all about."

"You have had a lot of trouble in your life, father. But you've never given up. Nobody else has ever been given the name 'Israel' by an angel, and that was because you simply wouldn't give up. I'm proud to have a father like that."

"Oh, stop talking nonsense, my son, and keep going with the story. *Your* story."

"Well, the butler forgot me for two whole years, so for two more years I stayed in The Pit, wondering what had gone wrong. But, of course, God had everything under control. At just the right time, it was Pharaoh's turn to have a dream that nobody could interpret. Actually, I think his magicians and wise men were a bit scared to interpret it. There were two different dreams, and both of them involved the good things of Egypt being consumed by bad things that Egypt would be ashamed to own. I think the magicians and wise men didn't want to suggest that Egypt could possibly produce such terrible things, because that would have reflected badly on Pharaoh and they were afraid of the possible consequences."

"I suppose that makes sense. So you went ahead and interpreted it anyway, and still made him happy to hear it? Glad and kneeling at your feet, eager to praise you? You have an amazing knack, Joseph!"

"He didn't really do that, but yes, I did interpret the dreams after God showed me what they meant – and Pharaoh believed me. I spoke as convincingly as I could, since I had to make him absolutely certain that I was right. They were the dreams that announced to Pharaoh the seven years of plenty we have had and the seven years of famine that we are now in the middle of. I also told him the best plan – God put it clearly in my mind – for dealing with the problem and saving Egypt from disaster. Pharaoh listened to my explanation and then appointed me as leader over Egypt to do the things I had suggested in my plan. Basically, we had to collect vast amounts of seed in the first seven years of plenty, so that when the bad years came, we would be able to live and not die."

"So how did you know what was needed to make it work?"

"God has given me abilities in strange things, father. Lots of things that I have never done before, I know that I will be able to do with his help, and when he tells me what to do, he always makes it so that I have the chance to do it.

"Do you ever think about just how much power God has? Putting me in Egypt at the right time and in the right way so that when he gave Pharaoh a dream, there was someone there to interpret it? And when it was interpreted, showing me the way to solve the problem. And then making seven fantastically fertile years during which the land of Egypt produced more food each year than it has ever produced in any three years before. The amount of planning needed and the power required to be able to bring it to fulfilment are utterly beyond my comprehension, father. Yet this is the God who chose our father Abraham and led him out of Ur to the land you have been living in. This is the God who loves us and has promised that Abraham's seed will be as many as the stars of heaven, and who has given you 12 sons to start it along the path.

"But father, the things I have been thinking most recently about the word of God and his plans are about the seed, the single seed that has been promised, the one who will own the gates of his enemies. This is the best promise of all and the one that I most look forward to. Who will this son be? When will he come? How will we know that he is the one who was intended by God as the special seed of Abraham? How long do we have to wait, father, and when will others recognise that this is *the* son of Abraham; the special one that God has provided as he said he would do? Mount Moriah. God providing. A son who will solve all of the problems of the world and love God as well."

Epilogue

Jacob enjoyed the company of Joseph and the bounty of Egypt for 17 years. The time of famine finally passed and Egypt resumed her normal cycle of ploughing and harvest, the blessings of fertility brought by the flooding of the mighty Nile.

Joseph continued as governor and Pharaoh basked in the reflected glory of an administrator who led Egypt to still greater prosperity under the guidance of El Shaddai, the God of the Hebrews.

Joseph had saved his family through his faith, and now at last his faith began to have a real impact on his brothers' attitudes. They still marvelled at his forgiveness and worried that it might falter once their father died. But it didn't, and the brothers enjoyed each other's company for many years after Jacob was buried in the family burial cave in Hebron.

Three of the brothers developed an especially close friendship based on a shared love of El Shaddai: Levi and Judah became changed men as the years passed, changed enough to even acknowledge that it was Joseph who had inspired the change.

But as the years passed, whether as a result of the years spent in horrific conditions in The Pit or because his work was finished, Joseph aged more quickly than his brothers.

As the time of his death approached, Joseph gave orders that showed how much his faith was a part of his character. He called his brothers together and said, "God will surely visit you, and you shall carry up my bones from here."

Simple words conveying a simple message: the children of Israel would return to Canaan when God gave the command, and when they did, Joseph's bones must go too.

Joseph had been dead about twenty years when Levi had a daughter. And, though no-one had any idea of the fact, it was to be her younger son whom El Shaddai would choose to lead his people out of Egypt in their long-awaited return to the promised land.

They did return. And the bones of Joseph, Rachel's son, went with them.

Free Download

Paul in Snippets

An 81-page PDF novelette by Mark Morgan.

The life of Paul painted from the Acts of the Apostles.

Get your free copy of *Paul in Snippets* when you sign up for the Bible Tales mailing list. As well as the eBook, you will receive a weekly email newsletter with micro tales, informative articles and special offers.

Visit **https://www.BibleTales.online/free-pins**

Bible Tales Online

Other books by Mark Morgan are available from Bible Tales Online.

Terror on Every Side!

The Life of Jeremiah

From a family of priests in the peaceful reign of good King Josiah, came a young man Jeremiah, bringing words from God to his people. It was no message for the fainthearted, either. It was a message of *Terror on Every Side!*

Volume 1 – Early Days
Volume 2 – As Good As It Gets
Volume 3 – Darkness Falling
Volume 4 – The Darkness Deepens
　　　(expected December 2018)
Volume 5 – No Remedy
　　　(expected July 2019)

Generally available as paperback, eBook and audiobook.

Micro-tales

Collections of short stories about Bible characters or events, available in paperback, eBook and audiobook.

- ***Fiction Favours the Facts***
- ***Fiction Favours the Facts – Book 2***
  (expected December 2018)

Upcoming novel

- ***Daniel, Man of Light***
  (expected May 2019)

Bible Tales Online continues to publish books. To find the list of currently available books, visit

http://www.BibleTales.online/books